Good-bye Marianne

by Irene N. Watts

Tundra Books

Copyright © 1998 by Irene N. Watts

Published in Canada by Tundra Books, *McClelland & Stewart Young Readers*, 481 University Avenue, Toronto, Ontario M5G2E9

Published in the United States by Tundra Books of Northern New York, P.O. Box 1030, Plattsburgh, New York 12901

Library of Congress Catalog Number: 97-62177

Canadian Cataloguing in Publication Data

Watts, Irene N., date
   Good-bye Marianne

ISBN 0-88776-445-2

I. Title.

PS8595.A873G6 1998   jc813'.54   C97-932437-8
PZ7.W37GO 1998

We acknowledge the support of the Canada Council for the Arts for our publishing program.

We acknowledge the financial support of the Government of Canada through the Book Publishing Industry Development Program for our publishing activities.

Design by Sari Ginsberg
Typeset in Goudy by M&S, Toronto
Printed and bound in Canada

2 3 4 5 6   03 02 01 00 99

For Renate,
and in loving memory of Ruth Marianne
and our parents

For their friendship and ongoing support, I wish to thank Julia Everett, Jennifer Jensen, Gay Ludlow, and the late Russel Kelly. I also wish to thank The Child Survivor Group of the Vancouver Holocaust Education Centre, and Elizabeth Ball, Artistic Director of Carousel Theatre, Vancouver, British Columbia.

Contents

The Math Test

One, two, let me through
Three, four, police at the door
Five, six, fix the witch
Seven, eight, it's getting late
Nine, ten, begin again.

Marianne had made a pact with herself that if she could go on repeating the skipping rhyme without stopping, even to cross the street, and all the way till she reached the school gate, she'd pass the math test. Math had always been Marianne's worst subject. She'd been dreading this day all week, but she was as prepared as she could be. Today she'd arrive at school on time, in fact, with time to spare. The rhyme was just an extra precaution.

The school clock said 8:20 A.M. 'Good,' she had ten minutes.

Why was the school yard deserted? Where was everyone? The front doors were shut. Marianne tried the handle – locked. She knocked, waited, and knocked again. Someone must be playing a joke on her. At last the doors opened and Miss Friedrich, the school secretary, stood in the doorway looking at her.

"Yes?" she said at last.

For some reason Marianne felt guilty, though she'd been so careful lately, being extra polite and not drawing attention to herself.

"Good morning, Miss Friedrich. I'm sorry to disturb you. I couldn't get in," she said.

"What are you doing here? I suppose you've come for your records?"

Marianne thought she was having a bad dream. "Don't you remember me? I'm Marianne, Marianne Kohn, in the fifth grade. Please let me in; I'll be late for math," she said.

"Wait here," said Miss Friedrich, and shut the door in Marianne's face. Marianne heard her heels clicking away. It seemed a long time before the clicking heels returned. The door opened and Miss Friedrich stood there holding some papers. Marianne could make out a list of names on the top sheet.

"You are to go home at once, Marianne. Here are your records."

"Why? What have I done? This math test – it's really important. I'm already late. There's choir practice today, and I haven't handed in my library book."

"You may give your library book to me." Miss Friedrich took the book and handed Marianne a brown envelope. She avoided looking at the girl. "Now go home. Just go home – I have work to do."

Miss Friedrich went back inside and the door shut. Marianne looked at her name on the envelope. People only got their records when they changed schools. There was something going on that she didn't understand.

A cold splash hit her cheek. She wiped it away, and saw that her palm was streaked with ink. The sound of giggling made her look up to the open first-floor window. Faces grinned at her. A second pellet, blotting paper soaked in ink, hit the sleeve of her school coat. The giggling turned to laughter.

Marianne relaxed – it was a joke after all. But what kind of joke? This wasn't April Fools' Day; it was the third Tuesday in November, and she was freezing out here. The school clock struck the half hour: 8:30 A.M. She heard the sound of a teacher's voice thundering, "That's enough, settle down." The window above her slammed shut. The school yard was perfectly quiet.

Marianne reached up to knock at the door again. It was then that she saw the notice. She read the typed words nailed up for everyone to see, and felt colder and more alone than she had ever felt in her whole life.

She ran out of the yard, afraid to look back; crossed the street without looking; and went into the park. The words of the notice resounded in her head, and she knew that she would hear them for the rest of her life.

The Park

M arianne needed time to think. The words she had read on the door were as clear as though they had appeared on a billboard in front of her:

AS OF TODAY, NOVEMBER 15, 1938, JEWISH STUDENTS
ARE PROHIBITED FROM ATTENDING GERMAN SCHOOLS.

Expelled because she was Jewish!

The sun came out, warming the gray winter morning, but not Marianne's icy fingers which were cramped from holding the envelope so tightly. She sat down on a bench near the deserted band shell, loosened the flap of the hateful envelope, and pulled out her records:

NAME OF PUPIL:	Marianne Sarah Kohn
SEX:	Female
DATE OF BIRTH:	May 3, 1927
ADDRESS:	Apartment 2,
	Richard Wagnerstrasse, 3
	Berlin, Charlottenburg
RELIGION:	Jewish
FATHER:	David Israel Kohn
OCCUPATION:	Bookseller
MOTHER:	Esther Sarah Kohn
	(nee Goldman)
COMMENTS:	Marianne has been a
	diligent pupil.
	A. Stein, class teacher

'Diligent?' Much good that did her. What was she supposed to do now, be diligent by herself all day?

There was hardly anyone about, just a few nursemaids with babies and toddlers. Even if there had been crowds, today she was going to do as she pleased. She'd sit down like a normal person; that would show them. She might even ignore the KEEP OFF THE GRASS sign and walk on it! Better not, that might get her arrested – Mutti would have a fit!

Suddenly Marianne remembered that she was not supposed to sit on a public bench, or even be in the park. She jumped up guiltily and saw that she'd been leaning against the now-familiar words: ARYANS ONLY.

Marianne sat down again very deliberately, her back against the hateful words. She unbuckled her navy schoolbag and rearranged the contents to her liking. She pulled out her lunch, and put the wooden-handled skipping rope beside her on the bench.

Marianne unwrapped the neat, greaseproof paper parcel that contained the cream cheese sandwich her mother had made for her that morning. Only a few hours ago Mutti's hands had held the bread. It was a comfort. She put the envelope back in her bag, next to her apple. She'd save the apple till later.

This was a horrible day. Marianne knew her mother would say something comforting like, "Things will get better – it'll probably just be for awhile – what fun it will be to study at home."

'Well, it won't.' This was one of the worst days she could ever remember, much worse than any math test, even worse than Mr. Vogel's sarcasm. She could just hear him in her history class:

"Now, Miss Kohn, as we are privileged to have a member of your race in our class, I am sure you could enlighten us by describing Bismarck's Child Labor Laws. No? I assure you the laws prohibiting child labor under the age of twelve were not designed for the sole purpose of permitting *your kind* to sit at your desk daydreaming! You will write an essay on child labor in Europe before 1853. Hand it in to me on Friday."

At least she'd be spared any more of Mr. Vogel's sneering remarks, and the sniggers at his mockery of Jews.

There were some nice people in the school though. It was really decent of Miss Stein to write that comment on her records. She didn't have to do that. She'd miss Beate and her jokes – like that time she'd put a fake ink blot on Miss Brown's chair before English class! Gertrude was really nice too. Last year she'd been invited over to her house for a birthday party. There'd been a magician who had made her laugh, even though he'd pulled a paper flag with a swastika out of her sleeve, and everyone had stared at her! Then this year, Gertrude had apologized for not inviting her again, because her parents had said it wouldn't be possible to ask everyone in the class. Marianne knew it was because some of the parents would complain if she came, but at least Gertrude had been brave enough to say something. Most kids didn't.

Marianne wished her father would come home. He'd been away since that awful night a week ago when Jewish synagogues, homes and stores had been looted and set on fire. He'd gone to check on the bookstore, phoned and said everything seemed fine, but next morning Mutti told her that Vati had been called out of town on business. So why hadn't he sent her a postcard for her collection as he usually did?

Could her parents be getting a divorce? She didn't think so, although they seemed to be arguing a lot lately, after she'd gone to bed. There was a girl in her class whose parents got divorced. She lived with her mother and hardly ever saw her father. Marianne couldn't imagine being without one of her parents for so long.

She noticed a tall thin girl, with yellow braids wound around her head, staring at her. The girl sat down on the bench beside her and asked, "Why are you looking so worried?"

"I'm not. I was just thinking about my father."

"I'd rather not think about mine," said the girl. "He yells at me all the time. He's a platoon sergeant in the army and thinks I'm one of his recruits! Hey, why aren't you in school? Don't tell me, I can guess . . . you forgot to do your homework, so you're not feeling well."

She seemed good at answering her own questions, so Marianne mumbled something about a math test. She didn't want to lie, or explain to this strange girl that she no longer had any need to make excuses to miss school, that the *Führer* had made the decision for her.

"I knew it. I'm taking the day off too. They won't notice. The whole school is practising for tomorrow's concert in honor of some important Nazi officials from Munich. My music teacher always says, 'Now Inge,' – I'm Inge Bauer, by the way – 'just mouth the words, dear, like this.'"

Inge contorted her lips in an exaggerated imitation of her teacher. "I've got a voice like an old crow, the worst in the sixth grade. I'm never allowed to sing. What's your name?"

"Marianne." Marianne picked up her skipping rope quickly, avoiding any more questions. The rope flew under her polished shoes and sailed smoothly over her short, straight brown hair.

One, two, let me through
Three, four, police at the door
Five, six, fix the witch
Seven, eight, it's getting late
Nine, ten, begin again.

Inge joined in effortlessly. They skipped together until they were out of breath, chanting the familiar rhyme, faster and faster in unison. They collapsed on the bench, at last, laughing. Inge said, "Phew, I'm starved. I left my lunch in the cloakroom when I sneaked out. Have you got anything?"

Marianne rewound the rope. "I've got an apple in my bag. Help yourself."

Inge opened the schoolbag eagerly, drew out the apple, and took a huge bite. The brown envelope slid from the bag to the ground.

"Oh, sorry," said Inge and bent to pick it up. She read the name out loud, "Marianne Kohn." Inge jumped to her feet and stood in silence for about three seconds, then spat out the apple so that Marianne had to jump aside to avoid the spittle. "Kohn, that's a Jewish name – you're a Jew. Can't you read?" She pointed to the sign. "The yellow benches are for your kind."

She wiped her mouth on her sleeve, and her hands on her skirt. Then she grabbed Marianne's bag, and threw it onto the path as hard as she could. She wiped her hands again. Marianne picked up her things and moved toward the bench. Inge screamed.

"Keep away from me, you hook-nosed witch. I hate you."

Then she pulled the rope out of Marianne's hand and threw it at her. The wooden handles just missed her face, but Marianne felt them strike her chin.

Marianne longed to slap Inge, to wipe that ugly look from her face the way Inge had wiped her hands. Instead, she picked up the rope and put it into her bag. She fastened the straps with trembling fingers. Marianne smoothed the scratched leather, then looked up at Inge. The blonde girl was still standing there like one of the park statues, her face carved in hatred.

Marianne knew that nothing she could say or do would make any difference. She wanted to say, "I had fun – you made me laugh. We were almost friends for a little while, and now you hate me. How did that happen? Because of my name? Because I'm a Jew? My father fought on the Russian front in the 1914 war. He fought for Germany. He's got a medal to prove it. I'm as German as you are."

Instead she walked away. She could feel her shame like the aching bruise under her chin. Her shame felt worse than the words Inge had hurled at her.

A park keeper looked at her sternly as she walked toward the gates. "Shouldn't you be in school, young lady? Everything alright?"

"Yes, sir. Thank you, sir."

Marianne walked on, her head lowered. She just needed to get home.

· 3 ·

Locked Out

Marianne reached the corner of her street and breathed in the familiar smell of Otto's shop. Her father always bought his newspaper there on the way home, and sometimes a cigar to smoke after supper.

She'd walked all the way home without ever looking up, once ignoring a cyclist's bell as she crossed in front of him. Mutti was always warning her to be careful at the Wilhemstrasse's busy intersection.

Home at last. Now she had only to avoid Mrs. Schwartz's curiosity. Mrs. Schwartz was the caretaker for their building. She lived in the ground-floor apartment facing the street. It seemed her life depended on knowing everyone's business! The slightest detail was of utmost importance to her, and she knew almost everything that was going on in the building, on their street, and even what was said behind closed doors. The mailman often paused on his rounds to have coffee with her.

Luckily, today she was not scrubbing the front steps, skirt tucked into her apron waistband. Nor was she peering from behind the spotless white muslin curtains on her gleaming windows.

Marianne opened the front door and tiptoed past Number One. She crept up the stairs, careful not to step on the polished wood surround of the new, green, stair carpet that was Mrs. Schwartz's pride. Marianne's apartment was on the first floor. She rang the bell. No reply. Oh well, she had her key. Mutti was probably out shopping. "Oh, please, come home quickly. I have to tell you now," whispered Marianne.

Marianne had tied a piece of blue ribbon to her key, so that she could find it quickly. She unstrapped her schoolbag, but couldn't see the key. She shook the bag's contents onto the linoleum, so highly polished by Mrs. Schwartz that the Misses Schmidt upstairs complained that it was more dangerous to walk along the hallway than to cross the Kurfürstendamm: skipping rope, math textbook, notebooks, pen, pencil, eraser, compass and ruler, sandwich paper for her mother to wrap up her lunch the next day. Of course, she wouldn't be needing one tomorrow; she'd forgotten for a moment. Marianne checked her pockets – just her handkerchief and emergency subway fare. The key must have fallen out in the park. Marianne didn't even want to think about going back there to look for it.

She felt the day would never end. She heard a clock chiming twelve noon. Was it really only four hours since she'd left home that morning? Marianne slumped on the floor, leaned her head against the apartment door and closed her eyes.

There might be a letter from her cousin Ruth today. She'd promised to write and tell her about the new school. How long would a letter take to reach Berlin from Holland?

It must be at least two weeks since they had the good-bye supper for the Fischers, just after the High Holidays. Auntie Grethe was Mutti's older sister. Her daughter, Ruth, was thirteen and, unlike Marianne, went to Hebrew school, so the cousins didn't see each other that often. Uncle Frank was much more orthodox than Vati. Marianne and her parents attended the liberal synagogue, but she and Ruth would miss each other all the same.

Uncle Frank had lost his job months ago, so this was a lucky break for the Fischers – for him to find a position as a furrier in Amsterdam. At that last visit they'd eaten roast chicken and apple cake, and Mutti had made good strong coffee. Then the grown-ups played cards and she and Ruth had done the dishes, being extra careful of Mutti's Rosenthal china that had been a wedding present.

The china was beautiful: thin white plates with gold bands around the rim, and a different design of fruit painted on each one. There were little side plates to match. Marianne's favorite was the sprig of cherries; Ruth liked the grapes best. Vati always used to pretend the grapes were real, and then acted disappointed when they wouldn't come off the plate. Of course, that had been when she was little.

Ruth and Marianne listened to Marianne's records in her room with the door shut, so they could talk in peace after they'd finished in the kitchen. Ruth said she couldn't wait to get away from Germany. Her friend Lilian's family had been picked up by the Gestapo. Her father's name had been on a list. The apartment had been given to someone else. Lilian never came back to school.

Everyone knew that the Gestapo came without warning, usually at dawn. Ruth told her that she had nightmares about being picked up. That's why she was pleased to go to Holland, even though she couldn't speak Dutch.

Surely Vati couldn't be on a list too? Was that why he was away? That couldn't be the reason. All he did was buy and sell books, and make jokes – usually the same ones, over and over. The shop never seemed to make much money. Mutti was just wonderful at making do. She and Marianne would look through the fashion magazines together and laugh as if they were the same age, and then Mutti would say, "Don't you think, Marianne, if I changed the buttons, and put a new collar and some pockets on my navy dress, it would look just like that model? I'll try it."

And then she'd get to work and have her mouth full of pins for days, and they'd have cold suppers, but there would be the dress, or the new winter coat for Marianne.

But Mutti didn't laugh so much anymore, in fact, hardly ever.

The other day when he hadn't made a single sale all day, Vati had said, "Books aren't so popular in the Third *Reich!*" He was smiling when he said it. Mutti had told him to be quiet.

"You never know who's listening, David."

Her father laughed, but he got up and closed the window all
the same, and drew the heavy blue curtains.

Marianne dozed. It was quite comfortable on the floor, warmed
by the midday sun shining through the hall window. A blaring
noise sounded, uncomfortably close.

"Hands up, you're under arrest, stand against the wall."

Marianne jumped up, pressed her back against the wall, and
slowly raised her hands.

"I'd say that worked pretty well, didn't it?"

In front of her, dressed in a tweed suit, the trousers ending just
below the knee, a peaked cap of the same material perched on his
red hair, stood a boy holding a motor-horn, and smiling the
friendliest smile she'd seen in a long time.

· 4 ·

Ernest

"Sorry to wake you up," said the boy, and laughed.

Marianne couldn't help joining in, though her palms were still sticky from fright. "You really scared me. I thought you were the police."

"Ah, guilty conscience I see," said the boy in an exaggeratedly deep voice.

Marianne changed the subject. "That's a terrific motor-horn. It sounds exactly as though a car were parked right beside me. Wherever did you get it?"

"From a kid in my class. We traded. I did his math homework for a week for it. He got it from his grandfather's old car. Here, try it if you want. Just press the black rubber bulb and the noise comes out from the horn. Can't you imagine driving along and having to hold the horn in one hand when you want someone to get out of the way?"

Marianne took the horn and gave one gentle squeeze to try it out, then three great blasts, before handing it back. She'd have Mrs. Schwartz up here if she weren't careful!

"Thanks a lot. It's wonderful – just like Gustav's in *Emil and the Detectives*. That's my favorite book. Is that where you got the idea?" said Marianne.

"Good deduction. Exactly right. I hope to be a detective one day. I'd better introduce myself – I'm Ernest Bock. Tourist from Freibourg, at your service." He gave Marianne a small bow.

"Hi, I'm Marianne. I live here. I mean not in the hall, but in there." Marianne pointed to her front door. "I lost my key."

Ernest said, laughing again, "I guessed that. I'm pretty smart at picking up clues too. You are lucky living in Berlin. This is my first visit. I've never seen so many shops and lights blazing, and cars, and flags waving. Fantastic! My dad gave me this trip as a birthday present. He works on the railway, so he gets cheap tickets. Yesterday when we were on the train from Freibourg, I was thinking of the part in the book where Emil falls asleep, and the man in the bowler hat steals all his money. I can tell you, I kept my hand on the motor-horn the whole time, and didn't close my eyes once."

"Did you travel all that way on your own?" said Marianne.

"Oh, no, my mother's here with me. We're staying with Mrs. Schwartz, an old friend of hers. They went to school together."

Marianne asked as casually as she could, "You mean Mrs. Schwartz in Number One?"

"Yes, I've hardly spoken to her yet. As soon as we arrived, she and my mother rushed off to some big department store for bargains. They won't be home for hours."

"Wertheim's, I should think," said Marianne. "All the mothers like shopping there."

"That's the one. They said I should keep an eye on things till they come back. That won't be till the stores close, I bet. I'm exploring; hope you don't mind."

"Of course not," said Marianne. "How long are you staying in Berlin?"

"I wish it was forever, but it's just for two weeks. My dad and my brother know how to cook only one kind of food – sausages – boiled, fried, or grilled. Anyway, can't miss school for too long. You know how it is. Have you got the afternoon off?"

"Yes. I'm off school for awhile." Marianne bent down to pick up her things, stuffing them into her bag. Ernest helped her.

"You are lucky. Tell you what – while you're waiting for someone to come home, we'll pretend I'm Emil. I'll sit here on the top step, and close my eyes. You have to reach into my pocket and steal this ten-pfennig coin without my hearing you. I'll sound the horn if I catch you."

Marianne said, "Alright, but let's start with just snatching the cap. You put it beside you, and I have to take it away without you hearing me. We can advance to more sophisticated crimes later."

"Excellent. You have first go," said Ernest, and removed his cap. He leaned against the banisters, and closed his eyes.

Marianne removed her shoes, then began to creep up behind him. Unfortunately, the glossy floor squeaked even under her light step, and Ernest blared the horn triumphantly.

They changed places. Ernest picked up Marianne's skipping rope and formed it into a lasso. He slid forward on his stomach, and gently curled the rope over the cap.

Marianne heard the sound of a button scraping on the floor, opened her eyes, saw the rope miss her ear by inches and capture the cap. She shrieked, "Stop, thief," squeezed the horn, and both children shouted with laughter. At that moment Mrs. Kohn opened the front door and, hearing loud voices, one of which was Marianne's, ran across the hallway and up the stairs.

"What are you doing on the floor, Marianne? What's happened to you? Are you hurt?" Mrs. Kohn was deathly pale, and she was gasping for breath.

"Mutti, calm down – we were just playing. I lost my key and couldn't get in."

Meanwhile Ernest had picked up the rest of Marianne's things, put them in the schoolbag, and handed the satchel to her. He raised his cap, clicked his heels together, and gave the same little bow.

"Mother, this is Ernest Bock – he's here from Freibourg on holiday. He kept me company," said Marianne. She did not look at Ernest, knowing she'd giggle if she did.

"I'm very pleased to meet you," said Ernest politely.

Mrs. Kohn smiled a stiff little smile – she still hadn't got over her fright. "Good day, Ernest."

"I'd better be going. I haven't had lunch yet. Good-bye Ma'am, 'bye Marianne. See you again."

"'Bye, Ernest. Thanks."

Ernest ran down the stairs, two steps at a time. He gave her a final motor-horn salute before disappearing into Number One.

"Tell me where he is"

As soon as they were inside the apartment, Marianne and her mother burst out talking at the same moment.

"Where were you?"

"I've been so worried about you."

Mrs. Kohn fastened the safety chain on the door, then turned and gave Marianne a hug. "I've been sick with worry, darling. I heard the announcement on the radio, and rushed out to meet you, but of course you'd left. Was it dreadful for you?"

"Yes." She wasn't going to pretend. The morning settled like cold rice pudding in her stomach. "At least I missed the test."

Mrs. Kohn hung up her coat on the hall stand and followed her daughter into the kitchen. She picked up the brown envelope Marianne had taken from her schoolbag.

Marianne sat at the kitchen table, one elbow leaning on the blue and white checked oilcloth. She brushed her arm, in its clean white-sleeved blouse, across her eyes. "I'm getting a cold."

Her mother sat down facing her. She studied the records. "Oh Marianne, this was so brave of Miss Stein. She could be in a lot of trouble for writing such a nice comment about you." She replaced the papers and put them in the kitchen dresser drawer. She arranged two honey cakes on a plate and poured Marianne a glass of milk. "Now tell me, how in the world did you lose your key?"

Marianne said, with her mouth full of cake, "In the park."

"The park! Marianne, you know better than that. Anything could have happened. It's bad enough just coming straight home from school. I'm sorry, darling, but you know it's not safe for us to be in public places."

Marianne chewed her thumbnail. She shivered, remembering Inge.

"I still don't understand how a key can fall out of a closed schoolbag," said her mother.

"It must have fallen out when I got my skipping rope. Sorry."

Mrs. Kohn was about to say more when she noticed Marianne's flushed cheeks. "I think you really are catching a cold. Just as well you're home for a few days."

"A few days! Don't you mean forever? Why can't we go to Holland? Then I could go to school with Ruth." Marianne knew she sounded spoiled and childish – she couldn't seem to help it.

"We can try. Don't forget it took Uncle Frank a long time to get sponsored by his new employer. It's very hard to obtain a visa these days. We have to wait our turn. Now, as for going to school – of course you're not going to miss school forever. Do you think we would let that happen? The Rabbi has called a meeting for this afternoon so that all the parents can discuss the situation. There are lots of things we can do – set up classes in our homes even – for those students for whom room can't be found in Jewish schools."

Marianne began to chew her thumb again, something she hadn't done since she was a toddler. She didn't want to go to Jewish school and have bricks thrown through windows, and stones hurled into the school yard. It wasn't that she was more of a coward than anyone else, but she just wanted to *be* like everybody else, that is, like the kids in her old school – some of them, at least. "I'm not going to sneak around and join some homemade class!"

"Marianne, that's quite enough. Whatever's got into you today? Now tell me – and please, darling, I'd rather you ate your cake instead of your thumb – who was that boy? When I heard you scream, I thought you were being attacked."

"Is that why you were so unfriendly to Ernest? I told you, Mutti, he's nice – we had fun while I was waiting for you to come home."

"Did he ask you anything? What was he doing in our hallway? He doesn't live here. For all we know, he might be from the Hitler Youth, checking out the building." Mrs. Kohn brushed cake crumbs fiercely from the tablecloth, then poured more milk for Marianne.

"I can't drink all this milk; it makes me feel sick."

"You can. Drink it. It's good for you. And this is no time to be talking to strangers. We know absolutely nothing about him."

"But, Mutti, he's staying with Mrs. Schwartz."

"Mrs. Schwartz! Marianne, think! He could be spying on us, reporting everything we say and do. You know Mrs. Schwartz doesn't like us living here, you *know* that. She's a Nazi party member."

"Mutti, please listen. I know kids. Ernest's not spying. He's alright. He's just here for a couple of weeks with his mother. We like the same book. He's from Freibourg. He's perfectly safe."

"Marianne, you have to understand, we aren't safe. No Jew is safe anywhere in Germany. Do you think there are no Nazis in Freibourg? The Nazis are everywhere. The *Führer* has said we are enemies of the people. We are no longer considered citizens. If we are attacked in the street, or in our homes, no one will help us. There are countries who will take us in, but only a few people at a time, and an exit visa costs a lot of money. So Marianne, until we can go, we must be very very . . ."

"I know, careful," interrupted Marianne. The caution was becoming a family joke.

Mrs. Kohn began to clear the dishes. "Hand me my apron, please." Marianne took the blue apron that hung over the back of her mother's chair, and tied it round her waist for her. She gave her mother's waist a little squeeze to show she understood. Marianne sat at one corner of the kitchen table and said as casually as she could, "Mutti, when is Vati coming home?"

Her mother turned on the cold tap to rinse the glass, and said without turning around, "I don't know."

"Why won't you tell me where he is? I'm not a baby."

"Marianne, I don't know. I mean it. But even if I did, I wouldn't tell you."

"Wonderful. You don't even trust your own daughter."

"It's not that. It's just if you know something, and mentioned it, or were overheard, and reported . . ."

"Mutti, I don't have anyone to play with, or to tell stuff to. Who would I talk to? I don't have any friends anymore."

"You were talking and laughing with Ernest just now, weren't you?"

"I didn't even tell him my full name! I've a right to know where my father is. He's not in prison, is he?"

Her mother took off her apron and folded it. "No, he's not. All I know is what I told you – he's away on business. Now, I *must* go, or I'll be late for my meeting. I'm supposed to be there at 2:30 P.M. We're all arriving at different times, so it won't look like a protest. I told you, didn't I, the government has forbidden more than three Jews to meet at one time, but this is an emergency."

Mrs. Kohn sighed, put on her coat and hat, and picked up her string shopping bag. She kissed Marianne's cheek. "I'll be home for supper. I'll make potato pancakes. Vati's favorite."

"What's the point when he's not even home?" Marianne said.

"Because it's important to remember. Have a nice afternoon, darling."

She left. Marianne fastened the chain behind her. The apartment still felt safe and warm and quiet. She sang the refrain of the skipping rhyme:

> One, two, let me through
> Three, four, police at the door
> Five, six, fix the witch
> Seven, eight, it's getting late
> Nine, ten, begin again.

As long as she was inside her own home, who could hurt her?

.6.

Heil Hitler

M arianne looked through the living-room window. The first snow of winter was coming down in great blobs, and settling on the square yard that all the tenants shared. The neatly dug flower beds, the two chestnut trees, and the narrow bench were already covered with a thin white layer.

Marianne hoped last year's skates would fit her, though the way things were going, she probably wouldn't be allowed to skate on the river Spree this year. The list of forbidden activities was piling up like the compost heap by the back fence.

An apron hung stiffly on the line. One of the Misses Schmidt (Marianne always found it difficult to tell the old ladies apart) hurried out with a shawl over her head, to bring in the washing. The scrawny cat, Sweetie, who wasn't in the least "sweet," picked her way daintily after her mistress, wanting to be let in out of the cold.

Marianne heard the back door slam twice. You had to give it a good tug in damp weather to make it close. The Schmidt sisters were elderly, their hands were gnarled with arthritis, and they never managed to shut the door properly the first time. Sometimes her father carried groceries up the stairs for them. When Mrs. Schwartz wasn't around, they'd be really friendly and stop to chat with her.

"Dear child, how was school today?"

Marianne would bob a curtsy – she knew the old ladies appreciated a well brought-up child.

The afternoon loomed endlessly. She turned away from the window and switched on the radio. Didn't the network ever broadcast anything but marching tunes?

Marianne sprawled on the deep couch. The room was getting dark and it was only half past two. She hoped her mother hadn't had any trouble getting to the meeting. The Rabbi's house was right next to the synagogue, which had been burned in last week's anti-Jewish demonstrations.

The Menorah gleamed on the mantelpiece. Hanukkah in four weeks, her favorite time of the year. She'd never forget that time two years ago in the synagogue when the Rabbi reminded the congregation that the festival was about more than gift giving, was more than a children's holiday. "Thousands of years ago, at another time of persecution, a small group of Jews fought against overwhelming odds, for religious freedom. The Menorah tells the world our spirit will never die," he had said. "Let Hanukkah be as important for us as Passover and Purim."

Marianne hoped her grandparents would come from Düsseldorf as usual. They'd all miss Uncle Frank and Aunt Grethe though, and without Ruth she'd be the only child at the table. Nothing stayed the same.

What was she going to do this afternoon without school to go to? There'd be lots of afternoons like this now. Would she always feel this restless? Maybe she'd read – work her way through every book in the room. Just last month her father had finished putting up another shelf to hold all the books he kept bringing home. Mutti complained she couldn't reach the top ones to dust. Soon they'd run out of wall space.

Marianne helped herself to a peppermint from the cut glass dish on the coffee table beside her. This wasn't too bad. Right this minute her class was cleaning up after gym, the final class of the day. She could imagine Beate and Gertrude planning the first winter snowball fight and, of course, looking very innocent when a teacher walked by.

"I hope Miss Friedrich walks right into a snowball!" Marianne spoke aloud. When she was younger, she and her father had built a snowman in the yard with bits of coal for eyes and a long carrot nose. She'd wound a muffler round his neck, and cried when the snow melted.

Marianne's first school photograph stood on the coffee table. She was holding a big paper cone packed with treats. The cone was almost as big as she was. Every child in the first class had one. Marianne remembered the feel of the shiny blue and silver paper, the stiff paper frill around the top, and the taste of the first chocolate. It did sweeten school, and she had loved it from that first day.

Five years ago, 1933. It seemed so long ago. The same year the Nazis came to power. Her parents talked of a time before the Brown Shirts, before the red flags with their black swastikas were hung from every building, before the anti-Jewish slogans were scrawled on every wall – JEWS NOT WANTED HERE.

She even remembered when school was different. Now kids refused to sit next to her, and she was hardly ever allowed to play with the others at recess. She felt humiliated having to ask permission to join them.

Every day there seemed to be another regulation that made life a bit harder for her. Instead of saying, "Good Morning" to the teachers, the class had to say "*Heil Hitler*," and raise their right arms to salute the *Führer*. She never knew what to do about it. She hated to join in, but she'd be in trouble if she didn't. Well, that was one problem she didn't have to worry about anymore.

Her grandmother always said, "Look on the bright side."

Marianne looked at the photograph of herself when she was six – hair cut in bangs straight across her forehead, a big bow stuck on top of her head. Why couldn't she have naturally curly hair like her mother? No, she looked like her father – skinny, with straight brown hair. She wouldn't mind having glasses like him – they'd make her look older!

The radio blared out the shrill voice, familiar to every man, woman and child in Germany: "One people, one country, one *Führer*."

'Thank goodness there's only one of him.' Marianne began goose-stepping around the room, her legs raised high in imitation of the military. She liked the way her navy blue skirt billowed out, and then fell back into tidy pleats.

Marianne switched off the radio and ran into her bedroom, the one place that had always calmed her. She loved her little room, especially since she and her mother had redecorated it for her last birthday. It held all the things she loved most: her teddy bear, skinny from so much hugging; the scratched oak desk that used to belong to Grandfather; and the bookshelf her father had made specially for her, along which marched a parade of glass animals that only she was allowed to dust.

The wallpaper was a very pale yellow, cream almost. It was covered with sprigs of tiny rosebuds, each one with a dark green leaf. Her mother had found a green silky material that exactly matched, and made a new cover for her eiderdown to replace the babyish pink one she'd had for years.

Marianne looked out of the window; it was still snowing. The people who lived in the house on the other side of the lane had their kitchen lights on. When she went on errands, they never said hello anymore – lots of their neighbors looked away when they passed by now.

Marianne drew her muslin curtains, and then opened her sock drawer. That's where she kept her money box. Today was a perfect time to buy her mother's birthday present. Mutti's birthday was only three weeks away and Marianne longed to give her something really special.

She kept her allowance (when she didn't spend it) in an empty cigar box that she'd wheedled out of her grandfather. Opa and Vati loved their Sunday Coronas. She lifted the lid and breathed in the rich "party" smell of the tobacco that still lingered in the box. Her mother and grandmother always made a big fuss of opening windows to get rid of the blue haze of the cigar smoke.

Marianne counted her money. She had seven marks. She'd been saving for a bike to ride to school, so she had much more than last year.

Marianne buttoned her new winter coat, put on a scarf and beret, and remembered the spare front-door key hanging on the hook behind the kitchen door. She locked the door and ran downstairs.

· 7 ·

The Christmas Market

Marianne stood on the front steps and stuck out her warm tongue to capture the snowflakes. The sensation of melting snow was almost as good as eating ice cream. Marianne turned around slowly, her face up to the wintry skies. She stopped when she noticed the curtains of Number One twitch, and became aware of a face partly hidden by the muslin folds. Staring. Eyes. Berlin was full of eyes. Everyone was watching everyone else.

The street was quiet at this time in the afternoon. She was debating whether to take a streetcar to save time, when she saw a group of young men in Hitler Youth uniform handing out pamphlets. One grabbed her arm.

"*Heil Hitler*. Here, sweetheart, take this home to your parents." He pushed the pamphlet into her gloved hand. She didn't dare throw it away, but walked on. A voice shouted after her, "Say '*Heil Hitler*' next time." Marianne heard them laughing, and the same voice said, "No respect, these kids."

What would they have done if they'd known she was a Jew? Marianne shuddered, remembering Inge Bauer. She still had a bruise under her chin. She pulled her scarf up around her face.

Marianne turned down a side street. "I won't run, I won't."

Her mother always said, "If I had a magic wand, I'd use it to make you invisible. Meanwhile, whatever happens, don't draw attention to yourself."

Marianne forced herself to continue her walk. She passed *Fräulein* Marks's ladies' and children's wear. The door was boarded up and a big sign on the glass said, KEEP OUR STREETS JEW FREE.

Marianne, hurrying past, slipped on the icy cobblestones. Trying to break her fall, she landed on her right knee. There was a hole in her woolen stocking, and she'd skinned her knee. It hurt.

The pamphlet she'd been holding lay face up in the snow. The headline glared at her:

THE JEWS LIE. BEWARE THE ENEMY.

Underneath was a cartoon of an old man wearing a yarmulke – the skullcap that orthodox Jewish men wore. The cartoon showed a face with a huge hooked nose and sidelocks.

Marianne was used to propaganda, to the ugly slogans she'd seen ever since she had learned to read, but she felt sick for a moment. It was a feeling she was getting used to. Was this what

Hitler wanted, to make kids feel they were hated and not wanted by anyone?

Marianne walked on. When she reached Taubenstrasse she heard footsteps behind her. Was she imagining that she was being followed, or were the Hitler Youth out to teach her a lesson? She knew they needed no excuse to twist an arm, or worse if you weren't one of them, and they were everywhere.

Marianne walked on for a few paces, listening. Then she stopped abruptly and looked into the window of a small leather-goods store. The footsteps stopped. Marianne walked more quickly. Her knee was bleeding; she could feel the drops trickling down her leg. There was a marketplace at the end of the street. There'd be lots of people there.

She felt a hand on her shoulder, and a voice said, "Don't be scared, it's only me." The sound of the motor-horn echoed in the quiet afternoon. Marianne whirled round. Ernest grinned at her. "I followed your tracks in the snow – watched you out of the window too. You're a fast walker. Did you hurt yourself just now?"

"I grazed my knee. It's bleeding a bit. You are cheeky following me. Why didn't you say something?" Marianne wasn't going to let this country boy do as he liked in *her* city.

"Don't be mad. I've got to practise tracking suspects if I'm going to be a detective. Now, hold out your leg. Go on – I've got my first-aid badge."

Ernest took a handkerchief out of his pocket and folded it into a narrow bandage. Marianne held onto the wall for support, and raised her knee. Ernest knelt in the snow and bound up her leg most professionally. He finished by tying the bandage with a reef knot.

"Thanks, that feels better. I knew I was being followed. I never guessed it was you, though. I have to buy a birthday present for my mother – you can come if you like," said Marianne.

"Shopping!" Ernest groaned. "That's all you women ever do. But I can smell something cooking, and I'm starved. Let's go."

Taubenstrasse led into a small square. Market stalls were set up, and a mixture of the most delicious smells filled the snowy air: hot chestnuts, gingerbread, fresh-baked rolls, oranges and vats of sauerkraut.

Ernest went straight to a sausage stall. A woman wearing a shawl over a man's overcoat topped by a huge white apron turned fat sausages on an open grill. They sizzled over the fire. The woman stamped her feet in her heavy work boots.

"Who's next?"

"We are. Two *weisswurst*, please," said Ernest. "Is that what you'd like, with mustard?" Ernest looked at Marianne. She hesitated for just a minute. She'd never eaten one before. She felt as if *she* were the tourist in Berlin, not Ernest.

"Please," she nodded.

The woman speared two sausages, spread them thickly with mustard, and put one in each of two crisp, white rolls. She gave Marianne the first one. "Good appetite," she said.

Ernest had grandly refused to let Marianne pay. She took a bite. Juice dribbled down her chin; mustard dripped from Ernest's.

They ignored the mess, looked at each other and laughed. No one took any notice.

Afternoon shoppers hurried to finish making their purchases before dark.

"What we need now . . ." said Marianne.

". . . is gingerbread," finished Ernest, eyeing a stall piled high with honey cakes, chocolate pretzels, gingerbread mice with sugar whiskers, and gingerbread houses, dolls and animals.

"My treat, but don't take all afternoon," said Marianne. "I still have to get my mother's present."

Ernest chose a gingerbread soldier with a chocolate sword, and Marianne said, "I'll have a tree, please." She handed over twenty pfennigs for their purchases, and began to nibble her way round the outline of the triangles edged with white icing.

One year she had passed Mrs. Schwartz's door, and had been allowed to peek at her Christmas tree. She'd never forgotten the fresh smell of the pine, and the bright ornaments hanging from every bough. The warmth of the candle flames, flickering in their holders on the branches, was the most magical thing she'd ever seen. Somehow, eating gingerbread in this peaceful square had reminded her of that.

Ernest, his mouth full, said, "This is absolutely the best gingerbread in the world, and I'm an expert, because my grandmother works in a bakery in Freibourg."

They walked round till they came to a stall selling carved walking sticks, wooden whistles, ornaments and toys. Marianne looked for something that would appeal to her mother.

"My sister, Anna, wants a doll from Berlin. Your advice will be gratefully accepted," said Ernest, trying out a walking stick whose handle was carved in the shape of an eagle. Marianne realised that Ernest was embarrassed to be seen looking at toys. She thought it was really nice of him to think of his sister.

"How old is Anna?"

"Nearly six. She's the baby in the family, so of course she's spoiled. She might like this." He pulled the strings of a ferocious-looking jumping jack.

Marianne picked up a small jointed doll with real braided hair, the golden ends tied in red bows to match the doll's skirt and the braiding on the black bodice. Her blue eyes and spiky eyelashes were carefully painted; her wooden face had a sprinkling of freckles, rosy cheeks and a mouth that looked surprised.

"Your little sister would like this. Look at the embroidery on the sleeves – it's perfect," said Marianne.

"You're right," said Ernest.

The doll cost three marks. While it was being wrapped, Marianne noticed a careful arrangement of music boxes. She particularly admired one which had a delicate carving of flowers on each corner of the polished wooden lid. The stall owner turned the key, and Marianne hummed along with the familiar tune. It was a lullaby her mother used to sing to Marianne when she was little, to comfort her when she awoke in the dark:

Sleep my baby sleep,
Your Daddy guards the sheep.

38

Mother shakes the gentle tree
The petals fall with dreams for thee
Sleep my baby sleep.

The man asked Marianne, "Do you like Brahm's 'Cradle Song,' Miss?"

"Yes. My mother taught it to me. She would love this music box," said Marianne. "Is it very expensive?"

"It costs four marks, young lady. It is my own carving."

Marianne gave him a five-mark note and said, "Thank you very much. It's a beautiful box – all your things are beautiful." The man wrapped the box, handed Marianne the change and said, "I'm glad my work will find a good home. Come back again."

The street lamps came on. A man trundled a wooden cart over the cobblestones. On it was a gramophone. The man turned the handle. A Wagner march filled the air. Ernest went over to him, and put a coin in a tin cup standing on the trolley.

"He says he's a war veteran – he's only got one leg," he said to Marianne.

The snow started to gently fall again.

"Let's go home," said Marianne, and they turned to leave. As they reached the edge of the square where the row of apartment houses stood, a scream of tires disturbed the winter afternoon.

· 8 ·

"Sleep my baby sleep"

A truck roared into the square. It skidded to a halt in front of a gray house, one of a row overlooking the market. Storm troopers carrying rifles jumped out, their glossy boots shining in the lamplight. One kicked over a basket piled high with apples, which was standing by the fruit stall. Apples rolled in all directions. The troopers hurried up the steps. A voice shouted, "Open up. *Juden raus.*"

Marianne was unable to move. She wanted to run, but she seemed to be trapped in one of those dreams where she could not make her feet obey her. Ernest gripped her arm, "There's going to be an arrest; this is my lucky day."

The sounds of breaking glass and splintering wood rang out over the square. A few people watched, like Ernest, wanting to know what was going to happen next. Mothers took their small children by the hand and hurried away. The fruit seller picked up his apples, and polished them one by one on his striped apron.

Marianne whispered to herself as much as to Ernest, "I have to go now. I'm going." She crossed the square. Away from the truck, away from the storm troopers, away from the sounds in the house, which the gramophone could not muffle.

"Wait, I just want to see what's going on," said Ernest.

Marianne wasn't listening, except to a voice in her head which was saying, 'Go home.' She turned her head, forced to do so by the sounds of glass breaking, a cry, the thud of a body landing on cobblestones.

The soldiers clattered down the steps and picked up the body of a man lying facedown in the snow. They dragged him to the truck and hauled him over the side. The truck pulled away, its tires spinning.

The square was quiet again. Drops of blood glistened, scarlet as winterberries, under the street lamp where the man had fallen. His black cap lay forgotten in the snow. People moved on.

Marianne began to run. Ernest sounded the motor-horn behind her. "Wait for me." He caught up with her. "I don't think he was dead," said Ernest, to comfort her.

A cold wind blew little flurries of snow against their faces. Ernest turned up the collar of his jacket, and Marianne pulled her scarf over her mouth. It gave her an excuse not to speak. There was nothing to say.

When they got home, Ernest said, "You look like a bandit with your face all muffled up. Good disguise. It was fun today. Thanks. See you." He disappeared into Number One.

As soon as Marianne was back inside her own apartment, she took off Ernest's bandage. Her knee had bled. She ran cold water and washed the handkerchief in the kitchen sink. The stain came out easily.

Marianne went into her bedroom and dropped her clothes on the floor. She put on her nightdress and lay down on her bed. Then she unwrapped the music box and turned the key. She sang the words of the melody:

> Sleep my baby sleep,
> Your Daddy guards the sheep.
> Mother shakes the gentle tree
> The petals fall with dreams for thee
> Sleep my baby sleep.

When the tune was finished, she put the box under her pillow, curled up under the covers, and slept immediately. She did not stir when her mother came in, folded her clothes, and quietly closed her bedroom door.

A Letter from Ruth

I t snowed all week.

Marianne opened her eyes. She stretched, sat up, and smiled at her mother, who stood beside her bed holding a tray.

"Breakfast is served, Your Highness."

"I'm not ill, am I?" asked Marianne.

"Just a treat," said her mother. "I *am* sorry I got home so late again last night. I'll make up for it with the best potato pancakes ever, for supper. Now, please eat your breakfast before it gets cold."

"I'm starved," said Marianne, tapping the top of her boiled egg. "Sit on my bed and tell me about the latest meeting. Will there be school classes for me to go to?"

Mrs. Kohn sat at the end of Marianne's bed. "First I have a surprise."

"Vati's coming home?"

"Not quite yet. But . . ." Mrs. Kohn put a thin blue envelope beside Marianne's cup of hot chocolate. "This is nice, too, don't you think?"

Marianne opened the letter, slitting the envelope with her knife in exactly the same way her father always opened his mail. "It's from Ruth! Listen . . ."

"107, Leidesgracht, Apartment 5
Amsterdam, Holland
November 14, 1938

"Dear Marianne,

"I'm writing my first letter to you in our 'new' apartment on the fifth floor of this skinny old building, which is at least two hundred years old. The house overlooks the canal. It's almost as good as living on a boat. I can watch everything that's going on – kids playing, people meeting, quarreling, flirting. Here is a sketch of our building; it looks foreign, doesn't it? There are furniture hooks on the outside of the house because the stairs are too narrow to bring up big furniture. It has to be pulled up by rope. Luckily my piano doesn't have to go through that treatment. I had to leave it behind, as you know. I hate to think whose sausage fingers will touch the keys.

"I do miss my music and lots of things about Berlin, but *not* . . . well, you know what. Papa is still worried that we are not far enough away. He listens to the BBC (the British radio station) all the time, and thinks there may be a war soon. Then what will happen to the Jewish people?

"Papa bought me a secondhand bicycle so I can ride to school and save money by not taking the streetcar. The school I go to is on Jodenbreestraat, the Jewish quarter, near the Rembrandthuis. I have lots of homework to do because, of course, I'm behind, not knowing Dutch yet. The kids are really friendly and don't laugh too much at my efforts to speak. I'm glad we took French and English at school, at least I can keep up in those classes.

"Marianne, it's so much better here. I feel free, almost like everyone else. The markets are wonderful. There must be at least a hundred different kinds of cheese. I'd love to send you some. Can't you just imagine Mrs. Schwartz poking the parcel and telling the mailman, 'There's something very funny in here. Sniff, sniff.'?

"I'm getting writer's cramp. I want a letter from you very soon, with news about everything you're doing. Love to Auntie Esther and Uncle David. Mutti is writing to them. A kiss for my little cousin.

From Ruth"

"What a lovely letter. I must answer right away," said Marianne.

"Yes, she does sound happy. But Marianne, please don't leave the letter lying around. Put it out of sight. Ruth writes too freely. She's forgotten so quickly how things are here."

"Mutti, no one but us is going to see it – no one ever comes here anymore." Marianne looked up and saw her mother's worried expression. She remembered the man in the market last week. "Of course I'll put the letter away, as soon as I've answered it. Thank you for my delicious breakfast. Now, tell me about the meeting – I can't wait one more minute."

Mrs. Kohn said, smiling, "Even ladies of leisure must get dressed. As soon as you're ready, I'll tell you. I'm just going to start clearing up the kitchen. Don't forget it's my day for volunteering at the orphanage." She left the room.

Marianne washed quickly, longing to hear her mother's news. She put on her favorite red and white wool sweater over a gray pleated skirt.

"I'm ready."

"How nice you look, darling." Mrs. Kohn put down her coffee cup and said, "It was a long meeting. People are worried and upset. It was mostly mothers there. So many men are in hiding, or . . ."

"Mutti, you can say it."

"Alright I will – or are in concentration camps. I'm sure they'll be released soon; it's just a question of time. Now, about school. The Jewish community is short of teachers, books, and space for all the children who can't go to German schools anymore. Some of the mothers prefer their children to be taught at home. They feel that's safer than allowing them to walk to the classes we'll set up. The Rabbi says room will be found for the rest of you somehow. It will all be sorted out in a couple of weeks.

Meanwhile, darling, you have your books here. You must try to carry on by yourself for awhile.

"Now, I must hurry to the orphanage. Wonderful news. The orphans are to join a group of more than two hundred children who will be allowed to leave Germany. They are being sent to England. Good homes will be found for them there. They're leaving in a few days, and each child must be packed and ready. Think of all those suitcases! It's like a miracle that they'll be sent to safety. The Rabbi hopes many more Jewish children will be taken in by countries wanting to rescue our children."

"But, Mutti, having to go so far away, how awful!" said Marianne.

"I explained to you before, we don't always know what will happen. The most important thing is for them to be safe."

Marianne flung her arms round her mother's neck. "Thank goodness I'm not an orphan. I'd never leave you and Vati to go so far away. You wouldn't send me away by myself, would you, Mutti? Promise me you'd never do that."

Mrs. Kohn kissed the top of Marianne's head and said, "When you've finished your letter to Ruth, why don't you come and pick me up at the orphanage, say about one o'clock? I like to walk home with you."

"I'd love to. You go now, Mutti, or you'll be late. I'll put the dishes away. And be careful."

"You're beginning to sound just like me. Thanks, darling. I'll see you later." Mrs. Kohn patted her daughter's cheek, put on her hat and coat, and closed the front door softly behind her.

England! Marianne had begun English lessons two years ago. She liked learning languages. She tried to remember what to say when asked, "How do you do?" Was it "very well" or "werry vel"? She could never remember. She tried saying it both ways, speaking aloud to her reflection in the kitchen mirror, "Tank you werry much."

The sound of a horn blaring sent her rushing to the front door. "Ernest, are you crazy? We're going to be in big trouble."

"I knocked on the door. Were you asleep?"

One of the Schmidt sisters leaned over the banisters and called out, "What's happening? Is something wrong?"

Ernest stuffed his fist in his mouth to stop himself from laughing. Marianne called out politely, "Good morning, Miss Schmidt. It's nothing. I'm sorry we disturbed you. Someone was showing me how his alarm system works." Miss Schmidt clucked disapprovingly. A moment later her door shut.

"Lucky Mum and Aunt Helga are out," said Ernest.

"Aunt Helga!" Marianne howled with laughter.

"What's so funny?" asked Ernest.

"I didn't know Mrs. Schwartz's name was Helga," said Marianne, and went on laughing. "I never even thought of her having a first name!"

"You've gone mad. Please excuse my friend, ladies and gentlemen." Ernest spoke to an imaginary audience.

"Do you want to come in for a moment?" asked Marianne.

"Thanks." Ernest followed Marianne into the kitchen. "I have to do this school project on the Brandenburg Gate. Like to go with me? Then, this afternoon, I'm meeting my mother. She says I need new winter shoes. She's taking me out for ice cream and pastries afterward, as a reward for good behavior."

"I have to pick up my mother as well, but I've got a couple of hours. Just wait a minute – I'll put on my coat. I'll get your hand-kerchief too."

When Marianne came back into the kitchen, Ernest was holding Ruth's envelope. "Here's your handkerchief; it's quite clean now," said Marianne. For a moment she remembered her mother's warning.

"Thanks. Could I have this Dutch stamp? I've already got it, but I could use it for a swap."

"Of course. Have the whole envelope. I'll just take out the letter." Marianne put Ruth's letter in a drawer.

"Thanks a lot. Let's go."

· 10 ·

The Parade

Walking along to the streetcar, Marianne felt completely happy. Ernest had said, "My friend is mad." 'My friend.' Perhaps everything would turn out alright after all. Vati would come home; she'd start school again. Things would get better. Everyone kept saying that.

"What are you smiling about?" asked Ernest.

"I'm mad, remember? So of course I smile at nothing at all. I'm really smiling, though, because I get to watch someone *else* do a school project."

"You Berliners have got it good."

Ernest made a face at her and they ran for the streetcar.

"Not in school?" the conductor commented cheerfully.

"I'm doing a project on the Brandenburg Gate," said Ernest.

"Nice-looking helper." The conductor winked at Ernest, and Marianne blushed. The conductor rang the bell and they got off just before the gate.

Ernest stood absolutely still. People moved around him. He stared first at the wide sweep of Unter den Linden, the avenue of parades and victory marches, that stretched through the center of the city. Marianne knew he was imagining great armies coming through the Brandenburg Gate. She had never really looked before at the twelve huge stone pillars supporting the gate, or at the Goddess of Victory above, driving her chariot drawn by four stone horses. A sea of red flags hung from the surrounding buildings.

"It's sixty-five feet tall," said Ernest.

"You tourists know everything." All at once it was fun seeing Berlin through a visitor's eyes.

The sounds of drumming and marching feet drew near. Led by a drum corps of boys wearing khaki shirts and black shorts and the armbands of the Hitler Youth, a troop of young men in uniform stepped in perfect unison toward Pariser Square. Behind them marched the girls' corps, in white blouses, blue pleated skirts and brown jackets. They stood at attention facing the small crowd.

Ernest grabbed Marianne's hand and pulled her right to the front of the crowd. His arm flew out in salute, and his voice rang out with those of the watching people and of the Hitler Youth, "*Sieg Heil. Sieg Heil. Sieg Heil.*" Ernest seemed to grow taller. He was a stranger. It was as if she had never seen him before.

Marianne stooped to tie her shoelaces. She stayed down, hoping not to be noticed. She'd do anything to get out of hailing the *Führer*.

"What's the matter?" said Ernest. "You'll miss everything."

Marianne stood up. The words of the "Horst Wessel" song echoed over the square:

> We raise our flag, our ranks in tight formation
> Our troopers march, with firm and even tread
> The spirit of our fallen comrades . . .

Marianne did not hear another word because at that moment, she looked straight into the shining eyes of the girl she had met in the park. It was Inge. She wasn't imagining it. She'd never forget Inge Bauer. Inge's eyes glittered. She seemed under a spell.

"I feel a bit dizzy," Marianne whispered to Ernest. She excused herself politely till she got through the rows of people, and then walked back toward her tram stop.

Ernest caught up with her. "What a shame to miss the concert. My mother doesn't like crowds either. Shall we find a bench and sit down a minute?"

"No, I'm fine, really. I have to meet my mother soon anyway. Please go back. You still have to do your project. There's my streetcar now."

"Good-bye then. See you later." Ernest raised his hand in a half wave and hurried back into the throng of Nazi worshippers.

'That was really nice of him, leaving the parade to make sure I'm alright.'

On the way home, Marianne sat hunched and small in her seat, trying not to be noticed, thinking about the way her life had changed so abruptly.

Every single day since she'd been forbidden to attend school, Marianne had forced herself to go for a brisk walk round the neighborhood. She was afraid that if she missed even once, she'd never leave the safety of her apartment again. She walked with her head up, but avoided the eyes of anyone in uniform. It wasn't easy because there were so many soldiers and police everywhere – marching, saluting, often dragging passersby into trucks and cars.

One afternoon, she joined a small group of people who were good-naturedly watching two boys fighting. Their local policeman, whom everyone knew, separated them. He was in a good mood, smiling and greeting some of the women by name.

The younger boy said to the policeman, "Please, sir, I left my bicycle leaning against this lamppost, and I was gone only for a minute to post a letter for my mother. Then when I came back, he'd taken my bicycle and he won't give it back."

The other boy, who was bigger, said, mimicking the younger one's voice, "Please, sir, this boy is a Jew. That's not stealing, is it?"

The policeman's mood changed abruptly. He cuffed the Jewish boy so hard, he hit his head against the lamppost. "You're getting off lightly," he said. "Next time you make a complaint against a citizen of the *Reich*, I'll take you into custody." The boy ran off, holding the side of his head.

As Marianne turned to go home, she heard the policeman chuckle and say, "You've got yourself a fine bicycle there. You tell your mother I gave it to you – confiscated goods from Jewish vermin."

The red and white flags with their ominous black swastikas, which hung from every building, waved in the wind with more menace than usual that day. They signalled a very clear message to Marianne – YOU AND YOUR KIND ARE THE ENEMY IN THIS LAND.

One dreadful morning a few days later, a woman whom Marianne knew slightly because she worked part-time in Otto's Cigar Store, saw her in the street and said, "Turn around and go the other way; go by the back lane. There's been a bad accident. A woman got killed when the Gestapo came and took her son away. Her body is still on the street." She'd taken Marianne gently by the shoulders and pushed her in the opposite direction because Marianne had been too shocked to move. That day, Marianne ran all the way home. She had quite forgotten she was not supposed to draw attention to herself.

How could the grown-ups say, "Things will get better"?

· II ·

The Quarrel

Late one morning, Marianne came back to the apartment. As usual, Mrs. Schwartz was on her knees polishing the entrance hall. It seemed to be her favorite place to keep an eye on the house's inhabitants. Marianne was sure she reported everything to her husband, who had recently been made block warden.

"Excuse me, please," said Marianne politely.

"Up and down, back and forth – you should be in school. How am I supposed to get my work finished? Don't put your fingers on the banisters; I've just waxed them." Mrs. Schwartz reluctantly made room for Marianne to get by.

Marianne managed to get inside her door with just a few dramatic sighs from Mrs. Schwartz. The telephone rang. Marianne hung up her coat. The telephone went on ringing.

"Yes?"

"Marianne, I've been trying to reach you all morning. Is something wrong?"

"Sorry, I went out for my morning exercise. Sound like a dog, don't I?"

Her mother seemed in a hurry, and did not give Marianne her usual warning about not going too far away from home. "It's better if you don't meet me at the orphanage today. We're all behind. I may be later than usual. Would you start getting supper, darling? Thank you. See you as soon as I can get away."

Marianne replaced the receiver. It was a relief not to have to go out again. Facing hostile streets more than once a day was becoming very hard, even though she loved meeting her mother who was now working almost daily at the orphanage.

Marianne made herself a cheese sandwich, and that reminded her that she hadn't replied to Ruth's letter. She got paper and an envelope from her father's rosewood desk, and settled down in the armchair to write to Ruth. There was lots to tell her . . .

"Apartment 2,
Richard Wagnerstrasse 3
Berlin, Charlottenburg
November 28th, 1938

"Dear Ruth,

"It was lovely to get your letter. Thank you. Sorry I haven't answered before this.

"Your new home sounds so quaint, (I've been dying to use that word). I expect you'll all be skating along the canals. Wish I could join you. Did you get new skates?

56

"I'm happy you've got your bicycle at last. I've decided not to save up for one just now.

"I have to change schools too. But I don't know where I'm going yet. I expect you heard what happened. Meanwhile, I'm not bored at all. There's lots to do.

"I met a very nice boy from Freibourg. Unfortunately, he's only here for a couple of weeks, but we're becoming good friends. His name is Ernest and he's thirteen. He and his mother are staying downstairs with Mrs. Schwartz (that's how we met). I found out old Schwartz's name is Helga."

Marianne smiled. The doorbell rang. She put down her pen and went to answer it.

"Who is it?"

"Me, Ernest."

Marianne opened the door. "Come i . . ." She did not finish the sentence. She felt sick and cold at the sight of Ernest in the full uniform of the *Jung Volk* – the boys' branch of the Hitler Youth – shirt with epaulets, black tie, brown leather belt and shining brass buckle embossed with victory wands. He wore the Nazi party armband.

"This is from Aunt Helga," said Ernest, handing Marianne an envelope addressed to Apartment 2. Marianne took it without saying anything.

"What's the matter? Are you in a trance or something? It's me, Ernest Bock, your friendly house detective."

"I didn't expect to see anyone in uniform," said Marianne in a voice not even she recognized.

"My mother's taking me out to tea. I *told* you before, remember? She likes me to look smart when we go out. I brought my uniform to Berlin especially. Next year I'll be promoted from the young people's group to the proper Hitler Youth. I can hardly wait."

Marianne spoke slowly and clearly so there could be no mistake. She did not lower her voice at all. "I'm Jewish," she said. She drew out her gold Star of David which she generally wore hidden under her sweater. The Star, on its delicate chain, shimmered as brightly under the hall light as did Ernest's belt buckle.

"I'm tired of hiding this."

Ernest said, "I've never met a Jew before. I mean, I never spoke to one before. I didn't know. Wait till I tell my brother . . . maybe I'd better not . . . he'd have to tell his group leader. Martin's sixteen; he's in the Hitler Youth."

"So!"

"Martin went to a rally in Munich last September. He shook hands with the *Führer.* Can you imagine? Shaking hands with the country's leader?"

"I suppose he's never going to wash that hand again," said Marianne bitterly.

"What's the matter with you? Of course Martin's proud of that. It was a great honor. Why are you so mad?"

Marianne said, "Why am I so mad? What's the matter with *me?* You come in here, dressed in uniform, showing off about your precious brother and your precious *Führer*. Don't you know what Hitler's done? He's stopped me going to school."

Ernest said, "Lucky you, that's nothing to complain about!"

Marianne said, "You don't understand. You don't understand anything. This isn't just missing a few days – it's never, ever going back. I'm eleven years old. I haven't finished learning everything. I'll be a person who left school after five years. When people ask me, 'And what are you going to be when you leave school?', what'll I say? That I've left already?"

Marianne looked at Ernest a moment, taking in his neatly brushed hair and polished shoes. "And another thing, look at you, cleaned up to go out somewhere special with your mother. I'm not allowed to do that. The restaurant wouldn't let us in, DOGS AND JEWS NOT ADMITTED." Ernest stood silent.

A voice shouted from the bottom of the stairs, "Ernest, I'm nearly ready. I want you down here in five minutes."

Ernest said, "That's my mother calling me. I know her idea of five minutes – ten more likely."

Marianne said more quietly, "My mother wouldn't dare call out like that; she's afraid to talk above a whisper in case she draws attention to herself. She walks in the gutter so no one can say she's taking up too much room on the pavement.

"I have no idea where my father is. The Nazis took away his business. For all I know, he might be in a concentration camp being punished and starved because he's a Jew. The Nazis smash Jewish shops, burn our synagogues, and the police don't do anything about it. Just stand and watch."

Marianne stopped. She was out of breath with an anger that she did not know she had inside her. Ernest's face was red, his fists clenched by his side.

"Now you wait a minute," he said. "I didn't start this fight, you did. My father was out of work for three years, but now he's working thanks to Hitler. Our *Führer* is making this country great again. If he says Jews are troublemakers, then he's right."

"Troublemakers?" said Marianne. "We don't make trouble. We spend our lives trying not to get into trouble. You don't know what it's like not daring to answer back, even if you're in the right; trying to make yourself small and invisible so you won't get hurt; being scared all the time; not wanting to tell you my name – Kohn – in case you found out I was Jewish."

Ernest stood motionless, listening.

"And how would you like it if one day you were told you had to change your name?"

"Great," said Ernest, "I'd call myself Gustav," and he sounded his motor-horn.

"Not choose," said Marianne, "ordered. One morning you wake up and your name is Sara."

"Sara's a girl's name," said Ernest.

"Oh, Ernest, you're being stupid," said Marianne. "Not you – you'd be called Israel. Your leader ordered all Jewish boys to be called Israel, and all Jewish girls to be called Sara. It was even on my school records."

"Sara's a nice name," said Ernest.

"But it's not what my parents chose for me. And another thing – no one ever helps us when we get pushed around, beat up. Just like that man at the market the other day. Did anyone help him?" said Marianne.

"Why should they? I expect he was a criminal," said Ernest.

"You mean a Jew, don't you?" said Marianne. "Your leader hates us; he said so and he wasn't even born here. We're just as German as he is – more."

Ernest's mother called angrily from below, "Ernest, I'm waiting. Come down this instant – I'm ready to leave."

Ernest stood up very straight. "You're a troublemaker – the *Führer* is always right. You're an ignorant Jewish troublemaking girl." He clicked his heels together, saluted, and said, "*Heil Hitler.*" He walked away stiffly.

When he was halfway down the stairs, Ernest pressed the motor-horn. It sounded like an insult to Marianne. She shouted after him, "You're just like all the others. You're all the same." Then she ran inside, slammed the door and fastened the safety chain. She stuffed the envelope into her skirt pocket and went back into the living room.

Marianne picked up the letter she'd started earlier and, without re-reading it, tore it up into very small pieces and threw them into the wastepaper basket. Tears ran down her face.

"To think that I told Ruth we're becoming good friends. I *never* want to see him again. I hate him. I hate them all," she whispered.

A Visitor for Supper

It was almost six o'clock before Mrs. Kohn arrived home. Marianne had finished grating raw potatoes, and was just starting to chop onions. She'd set out flour, salt, eggs, and milk, and had put the heavy frying pan on the stove.

"You get my award for daughter of the year," said Mrs. Kohn, and kissed Marianne. "I honestly don't know how I'd manage without you. Can you believe we were four suitcases short, so someone had to go and buy them? That was just one of the problems. Each child needs changes of warm clothes. They can take only what they can carry themselves, so that means the little ones have to leave behind favorite blankets or toys. Well, the socks are all darned, the shoes polished, the children's hair washed. Sixty orphans will leave from Friedrichstrasse Station on December 1st. It *must* go smoothly."

Mrs. Kohn beat the eggs before folding potatoes and onions

into the flour. Marianne wiped her streaming eyes. "Onions always make me cry," she said.

"Vati's favorite supper," said Mrs. Kohn.

The telephone rang. Mrs. Kohn wiped her hands on her overall. "What is it this time – surely not another crisis?" She went into the hall to answer the telephone.

Marianne set the table. Mrs. Kohn came back into the kitchen. Her cheeks were pink.

"Put the water on for coffee, then stand in the hall. Don't turn on the light. Take the safety chain off. When you hear a tap on the door, open it, and fasten the chain again."

Marianne looked at her mother's face and did exactly as she was told. Three minutes later she stood in the dark hallway, listening for the knock. She could smell the onions frying, and hear the crackle of hot oil.

There it was. She opened the door. A tall, thin figure came in, closed the door, and held her so tightly she couldn't have screamed even if she'd wanted to.

"Vati!"

"Marianne, I've missed you so much."

"Don't ever go away again."

Marianne took her father's hand and held on to it, even while she secured the front-door chain with her other hand. "Mutti, he's home. Vati's back."

By the time her father was seated in his usual chair, sipping coffee from the blue cup that only he was allowed to drink from, her mother was serving up the perfectly browned pancakes.

"I could smell those latkes right across Berlin," said Mr. Kohn, helping himself to applesauce.

"I had to bring you home somehow," said his wife, smiling. No one spoke for a few minutes, but Marianne was too excited to eat much.

"Are you home for good now, Vati?"

Her father said, "You are old enough to understand what's happening in Germany, and old enough to be told the truth. I know Mutti agrees with me. I've had to go underground."

"You mean like in subway stations?"

Her father didn't laugh. "Sometimes," he said. "It means I must keep moving, never staying in one place very long. Many people have managed to escape the Gestapo by just walking the streets. Berlin is a big city. I've not come close to being picked up again."

Marianne said, "I don't understand. What do you mean *again*?" She stared at her father's hands – usually so cared-for, hands which loved to hold books. The knuckles were swollen and mis-shapen – the skin cracked and split.

"After the terrible night of the fires and looting on November 9th, I was picked up with thousands of other Jewish men. Boys, grandfathers – young and old – marched to Sachsenhausen concentration camp on the outskirts of Berlin. They struck us with whips as we went through the gates."

Marianne held her breath. She didn't want to miss a word of her father's story and yet, she was afraid to hear what had happened next. Her mother said, "David, must you speak of this now?"

Her father continued, "We stood in the yard naked. It was freezing cold. It began to snow. Not everyone survived the night. Next morning, some of us were released. By a miracle, I was one of the lucky ones. I think, perhaps, by mistake. Things were very confused that day. For the moment, until things change in this country, I have to rely on friends and kind people to hide me."

"I still don't understand why you can't stay here," said Marianne.

Her mother said, "The Nazis have lists. They know the name and address of every Jew in Germany."

"My name is on another list as well – I'm especially wanted, you see – popular man, I suppose, charming, intelligent . . . "

Marianne could see her father was trying hard to make one of his jokes. "Please go on," Marianne said. "I need to know."

Her father continued, "When Hitler forbade Jews to own a business, I sold the bookshop. After the new owner took over, he found some books written by banned authors. It was very careless of me. The man reported me. So now, the Gestapo would very much like to re-educate me in one of their concentration camps. That's why even Mutti doesn't know where I am at any time. There, I've told you everything. Don't look so sad, both of you. I have good friends, and I feel sure that any day now, permission will come through for all of us to travel to another country. Who knows, next year we might be in Holland or England or Jerusalem or, perhaps, Canada or the United States."

Mrs. Kohn put the last pancake on her husband's plate, poured more coffee for him and a glass of milk for Marianne. Mr. Kohn ate quickly. "I must go. I'm just going to change into warmer clothes and dry shoes. Back in a moment." Her parents left the kitchen together.

Marianne cleared the table, and ran hot water into the washing-up bowl. She needed time to think over what her father had told her. What if he was caught again and sent back to a concentration camp? Why hadn't her mother told her all this?

"I'm not a baby," she muttered into the sink. "Why wasn't I told before?"

Her parents came back.

"Be brave, both of you. I love you very much. We'll be together again, even if, for now, it's only in our thoughts. Remember, not even Hitler can prevent that." Mr. Kohn hugged Marianne.

"See you soon. I love you, Vati."

Her parents went into the hall. She heard the front door close and the chain being replaced. "I'll finish in here," said her mother. "No more chores for you today. We'll have a cosy evening. You get into your nightdress, and I'll light the fire in the living room."

"Let's have a game of dominoes – we haven't played that in ages," said Marianne. She would be just as brave as her mother!

Marianne went into her room and changed. Then she opened the bedroom curtains. The sky was black and clear with a few stars shining over the city streets. The yard was white and clean with snow. So peaceful.

Mrs. Kohn had the fire going. A few pinecones gave off a woody smell. "If I close my eyes, I'm back in the forest with my mother. When I was a little girl, we'd pick blueberries and mushrooms and walk for miles through the trees."

Marianne got the box of dominoes down from the bookshelf. Her grandfather had made the brown wooden box. It was very plain, but the pieces inside were of real ivory, black-and-white. Her father had played with them when he was a boy. They played three games and Marianne won two. She yawned.

"Time for bed. Goodnight, my darling, sleep well. Everything will come out right in the end. I'll just sit by the fire a little longer."

Marianne went to bed. After awhile, she heard her mother's door close. She couldn't sleep. She went over everything that had happened that day. She closed her eyes. There was a Ferris wheel going round and round in her head, and she was on it. When she reached the top she was happy, but the wheel never stayed still long enough before turning again, so the happiness didn't last. She could see it, but she couldn't hold on to it.

Marianne slid into sleep.

· 13 ·

Gestapo

"Open up. Gestapo."

Marianne and her mother collided in the entrance hall. Mrs. Kohn whispered, "Ruth's letter." Marianne disappeared.

"Open up."

The sound of a rifle butt against the door.

"I'm coming."

Marianne heard her mother open the door. The slap of leather on skin. A stifled gasp. Marianne stood in the doorway of her room. She watched the Gestapo officers, their uniforms as black as the night sky, invade their rooms.

Mrs. Kohn put her finger on her lips. Her face was very white. She waited. Marianne stood without moving, watching her mother. Cupboard doors slammed. Drawers crashed. They heard glass shatter. Something ripped. Gleaming black boots walked toward Marianne. She edged back into her room, picked up her teddy bear, held him tightly.

The officer patted Marianne's head. Turned away.

"Let's go."

They left. Their boots rang out through the building. A car door shut, the roaring engine disturbing the dawn.

Marianne and her mother did not stir until the only sound they could hear was their own breathing. Mrs. Kohn closed the front door, fastened the chain. She and Marianne held each other for a long time.

"My hair – he touched my hair. I feel sick."

"We'll wash it. It's all over now."

"What did they want? Were they looking for Vati?"

"Who knows . . ."

"I hid Ruth's letter."

"Where?"

Marianne kicked off her slipper. The folded letter clung to the sole of her foot.

"You were very brave, Marianne. Now we'll burn it. Come."

Hand in hand, Marianne and her mother walked into the living room. The room looked as if a tornado had hit. Every single book had been dragged off the shelves, and lay on the floor. All her father's beautiful books were scattered, bent, facedown, the pages ripped. His desk was gashed, his chair snapped in two. The Menorah was in the fireplace, buried in cold gray ash. The box that held the dominoes was broken, the pieces strewn on the carpet. Slashed curtains hung like untied hair ribbons. Marianne reached for the Menorah, wiped it on her nightdress. Then she picked up the dominoes.

Mrs. Kohn went into the kitchen. Marianne followed her. It was better to look at the damage together. The glass doors of the dresser and most of the crockery were smashed. The Rosenthal dinner plates were in shards. The plants on the window ledge were overturned, the soil trodden into the floor.

Mrs. Kohn picked up a box of matches and a soft cloth. She took Marianne's icy hand, and they went back into the living room.

"I'm going to get the fire going." She pushed the duster into Marianne's hands. The ashes clung to the decorative crevices and ornamental curves of the Menorah's silver base. The feel of the cloth restoring the shine calmed Marianne.

Mrs. Kohn twisted some papers tightly, lit a match and burned Ruth's letter. She added pieces of splintered wood from the broken desk chair. Next she began to sort the books, smoothing the crumpled pages lovingly. Daylight crept into the room.

"It's nearly seven," said Marianne. The mantel clock went on ticking in spite of a crack across the glass.

"I'm going to make us some coffee. You'd like that, wouldn't you Marianne, with lots of hot milk?" Marianne nodded and her mother left the room.

What could she do for her mother? What would make them both feel safe again?

Marianne remembered the gift she'd bought at the market. It was still hidden at the back of her underwear drawer. She ran to get it. Then she waited by the fire for her mother.

Mrs. Kohn came into the living room carrying a tray. She sat on the floor beside her daughter, and handed Marianne a cup of delicious, sweet, milky coffee. The cups did not match, and one had a handle missing.

"Mutti," said Marianne, "we're going to pretend that today is your birthday."

"I can't think of one reason why I'd want to be thirty-seven even one day sooner than necessary."

"Well I can," said Marianne. "I think you need a present." She put the parcel in her mother's lap.

"What pretty paper; it's much too nice to throw out."

Whenever Mrs. Kohn received anything wrapped in gift paper, she always said exactly the same thing. It used to drive Marianne and her father crazy, because they liked to tear the paper off quickly and get to the present. Today Marianne didn't mind at all.

At last Mrs. Kohn finished. She drew out the box. Her fingers traced the carved flower design gently. She turned the key. Brahm's "Cradle Song" filled the room. Marianne sang the words softly:

Sleep my baby sleep,
Your Daddy guards the sheep.

Mother shakes the gentle tree
The petals fall with dreams for thee
Sleep my baby sleep.

Mrs. Kohn said, "I will never part with this. It's the most beautiful gift anyone has ever given me. Thank you, Marianne."

They finished their coffee, and set to work to clear up. By ten o'clock all the broken china and glass had been swept up, books were neatly stacked, and those that could be repaired put in a box. Marianne had washed her hair and sat down to a late breakfast with her mother.

"I'm glad they didn't find your homemade black cherry jam," said Marianne, spooning some more onto her bread.

"I was thinking we could cut up the bedspread from the spare bed. That would do for curtains, don't you think?"

"Yes," said Marianne, with her mouth full. "What else do we have to do?"

"Would you mind going to the bakery for our breakfast rolls? Mr. Altmann will wonder why we haven't picked up our order. I'm going to scrub this floor, and then wash all the clothes in my room. They're still on the bedroom carpet. The Gestapo threw everything out of my wardrobe."

"I'm finished eating. I'll go right away." Marianne put on her coat. Something rustled. The envelope that Ernest had delivered the day before was still in her skirt pocket. She must have put it there after their quarrel.

"Mutti, I'm dreadfully sorry, I forgot to give you this note from Mrs. Schwartz."

"It doesn't matter. Hurry back, darling. Oh, and take fifty pfennig from my purse for shopping."

"Good-bye. I'll come home as fast as I can."

· 14 ·

"It's not so easy to close me down"

It was good to be out in the fresh air, away from the terrors of the night. Out here, things seemed to be normal. Marianne passed a few morning shoppers with their string bags on their arms.

She loved going to the bakery; it had always been one of her favorite chores. It was the first errand she'd ever been entrusted to go on alone. She had only been seven then and her mother had waited at the corner for her the whole time she was gone. Mr. Altmann never let any child leave his bakery without a taste of something warm and delicious, fresh from the oven.

At the corner of the Schillerstrasse, a familiar name was gone. FAMILY SAMUELS, FAMILY SHOE REPAIRS, had been replaced with a new name – BAUM, SHOE AND BOOT REPAIRS. NEW OWNER. ARYANS ONLY.

Who would mend their shoes now?

Marianne reached the bakery and saw her face reflected in

the window, splintered like the broken glass in the door. The heavy, wooden door frame was badly gashed, and the sign on the door said, CLOSED. A pile of shattered glass had been neatly swept up beside the step, which had dark stains on it. The display case was bare.

Marianne saw Mr. Altmann washing down the counter, and knocked on what was left of the door. Mr. Altmann looked up, smiled and walked toward her. For the first time since she'd known him – all her life, really – he looked old. His forehead had been clumsily bandaged; a little trickle of blood had seeped through the material and dried.

Mr. Altmann unlocked the door, and then quickly bolted it again.

"I don't know why I do that; habit I suppose. Don't look so worried, Marianne, it's nothing."

"Did they close you down?" Marianne asked.

"Temporarily. It's not so easy to close me down, even if they do break the glass. Close me down? No. Your mother, is she well? And your father, he is away on business, I hear."

"The Gestapo came last night, looking for something, but we are all fine now, thank you. What happened to you, Mr. Altmann?" Marianne said.

The baker began to sweep the floor.

"The usual things. This time a little more boisterous, perhaps. So they break a little glass, smash an old man's head. Mostly, the police look the other way. This morning they joined in."

Marianne said, "Some people leave."

"Not me. My grandfather built this shop. I use the same oven he did. I was born here, and here I stay. I can wait out a little madness, wait for things to get better. Don't look so sad. I'm going to fetch your breakfast rolls right now. The Gestapo didn't spoil everything."

When Mr. Altmann came out of the back room, he held a brown bag in one hand, and a triangular-shaped pastry in the other. "A little taste – warm from the oven."

"That's a hamantasch," said Marianne, "Purim's three months away. Why are you baking those now?"

"Because from now on the festival of Purim will be celebrated in my shop all year round. I want my customers to remember the brave Queen Esther and her Uncle Mordecai. I want them to remember how a tyrant, who tried to kill the Jewish people, was defied."

Marianne interrupted, her mouth full of the pastry Mr. Altmann had given her. "I love Purim. It's such fun to shout and clap in the synagogue, and wave noisemakers when Haman's name is mentioned. What a wonderful idea," said Marianne, licking the last of the jelly from her fingers.

"Exactly," said Mr. Altmann. "After the cruel Haman's death, the Bible says, 'The Jews had light and gladness, and joy and honor.' I wait for that time to return."

Marianne said, "I know a boy who has a motor-horn. It would make a wonderful noisemaker, but he'd never let me borrow it. He can't wait to join the Hitler Youth. I thought he was nice at first – kind, and fun – but they're all the same."

Mr. Altmann smiled at Marianne, and his eyes looked very bright, even through the cracked lenses of his spectacles. "It's hard to speak out, to be one voice against so many, but there are always some if you listen hard enough. Not everyone is a hoodlum.

"Keep well, child. My regards to your mother. And Marianne, remember what happened to Haman? We know another tyrant whose name begins with the same letter, don't we?"

Mr. Altmann made the sign of the letter *H* on the damp counter, and then quickly erased it with his cloth. He winked at Marianne. Marianne winked back, and stood on tiptoe to kiss Mr. Altmann's lined cheek.

"Good-bye, be careful," she said.

Marianne walked out of the shop, her head held high, and Mr. Altmann watched her until she was out of sight. Then he turned the CLOSED sign to OPEN, and waited behind the counter for his customers.

· 15 ·

Measles

When Marianne came back with the breakfast rolls, her
mother was still sitting at the kitchen table. Her eyes
were red. She pushed Mrs. Schwartz's note across to Marianne. It
read:

AS OF DECEMBER 10, 1938
JEWS ARE PROHIBITED FROM LIVING IN THIS BUILDING.
PLEASE VACATE APARTMENT TWO BY DECEMBER 9TH.
AT TWO O'CLOCK.
HEIL HITLER

   HELGA SCHWARTZ

Marianne said, "She can't do that. That's just a few days away."
Mrs. Kohn blew her nose. "Sorry, darling. She can. It solves
some problems, really. I've been thinking we should visit

Düsseldorf – spend some time with Oma and Opa. They'd feel safer having us there. You can share my old room. It will be good to be together in these dreadful times."

"What about Vati – how will he know where we are? What will happen to our things? Will I go to school there?"

"I'll get word to Vati somehow. Things can be replaced. They really aren't so important right now. Perhaps the Schmidt sisters would store some of our furniture. They've always been friendly to us.

"As for school, I'm sure the Düsseldorf community will arrange classes for Jewish children. Opa will find out for us. Think what fun it will be to live in the house where I grew up. I'll fetch our suitcases."

Marianne hugged herself joyfully. How wonderful to go on a trip with her mother. Of course she'd miss her room, but Oma always let her sleep in the little attic, "the ship's cabin" Opa called it. You could see the whole garden from there. All the fruit trees. Oma would have finished bottling the apples and plums, and would make plum tart, Marianne's favorite, sprinkled with golden-brown sugary pastry crumbs. Absolutely no one in the whole world made plum tart as delicious as Oma's.

Marianne loved taking Wolf, Opa's German shepherd, for walks. He was nearly as old as she was. He growled if anyone even looked at her!

She'd take her favorite books, her new green bedspread, her collection of glass animals – there were ten now. Her postcards, and of course all her clothes, especially her new green velvet "best dress" with the lace collar. Oma loved to see her grand-daughters dressed up.

Marianne heard the telephone ring, and her mother's voice. A few minutes later, Mrs. Kohn came running into the bedroom. She took Marianne's hands and whirled her around the room before collapsing, breathless, onto the bed.

"A miracle. Listen, Marianne, that was Mrs. Rabinovitch on the telephone. You know, the supervisor at the orphanage. Two of the children have measles."

"Mutti, you call *that* a miracle? Are you feeling alright?"

"Don't you understand? This means the girls can't travel. They will have to wait for the next transport. You've been offered one of their places. It's all happened so quickly, I can't believe it. I have to give Mrs. Rabinovitch our answer in ten minutes."

"Mutti, what about you? Are you coming too? And Vati? How can we leave him behind? What will we tell Oma and Opa? Ten minutes? I'd need ten years to decide something like that. Mutti, how can we leave everyone and everything behind?" Marianne was walking up and down her room, her thumbnail in her mouth.

"Marianne, listen to me. No, don't turn away." Mrs. Kohn took her daughter's hands in hers. "Look at me, darling. We don't have weeks or days to decide. We don't even have hours. This trans-port is a rescue operation just for children. A *Kindertransport*. The grown-ups must wait their turn. There are bound to be other opportunities for us to leave."

Marianne pulled her hands free. She was almost incoherent.

80

"You mean, I have to go by myself? No! Absolutely no. I'd have to be crazy to agree to something like that. I won't leave you all. How can you even *think* of asking me that? Mothers don't send their children away. Why did you say you don't know how you'd manage without me if you didn't mean it? Well, I mean it. I can't manage by myself. Who would I tell things to, some stranger? Who'd wake me up to go to school? Who'd nag me, and tell me to be careful when I go out? Anyway, I refuse to be an orphan. I refuse to go. I'd miss you too much." Marianne slumped down on the bed beside her mother, biting her nails.

Mrs. Kohn took Marianne's hand and held it tight. "We all have to learn to say good-bye to people we love, and there never seems enough time to prepare. But I am prepared to live without you, if it means giving you a future."

Marianne said, "I don't believe you. I won't say good-bye to you, and that's final."

Mrs. Kohn said, "Marianne, I think you have to. You see, I can't keep you safe anymore. I don't know how. Not here in Berlin, not in Düsseldorf, or anyplace else the Nazis are. You need to live a normal life, to go to school, to have friends over. To play and walk anywhere you want. How can I let you stay in a country where you dread a knock on the door; where we are afraid to light our Sabbath candles; where our houses of prayer are destroyed? I don't want you to grow up afraid because you are Jewish. Germany is a bad place to grow up in right now. One day it may be safe to live here again. For now, we must take this chance for you to escape to a free country.

"Vati asked us to be brave. Marianne, help us both to be brave enough. Agree to leave."

"Vati said we should look after each other, remember? I can't do that if I'm away from you," said Marianne.

"Can't you see how hard this is for me?" Mrs. Kohn tried to smile. "If you go to England first, it will be easier for Vati and I to follow you. It will mean we'll already have a foothold in a new country. It could make it easier for us to get an exit visa."

Marianne said, "On one condition. You must swear to come."

Her mother said, "How can I do that? But I solemnly swear to try. Marianne, there is no time left. What is your answer?"

"Alright, I'll go." Marianne put her pillow over her head so as not to hear her mother leave the room to telephone Mrs. Rabinovitch.

· 16 ·

Packing up

The rest of the day passed much too quickly. Marianne began by piling all her "must-take-this" belongings on her bed.

Mrs. Kohn said, "Two steamer trunks wouldn't be big enough for all of this. Look, I've made a list. The glass animals would really be safer at Oma's, don't you think?"

The pile on the bed swayed.

"The Tower of Pisa's falling," said Marianne. She started to laugh and then looked at her mother. They spoke at exactly the same time.

"I don't want to choose, I love my things. I don't want to go."

"I never want to finish packing, or see you shut this suitcase," said Mrs. Kohn. And then they hugged each other tightly.

Marianne thought, 'I'm really saying good-bye. This is good-bye, and I don't understand how it all happened so quickly. It's a horrible dream, and I want to wake up.'

"Why don't we pretend you're going away to a holiday camp? It's true in a way. Campers can only carry one suitcase because it's a long way to the campsite, and there's no one to help."

"Is that what the Nazis said? I don't mean the part about camp, more likely to be a concentration camp." Marianne immediately wished she hadn't made the flippant remark. She was always doing that lately, but it helped her to bear things more easily. Her mother's ashen face made her realize this wasn't the right time, but Mrs. Kohn answered Marianne as if she hadn't noticed the cruel reference.

"Yes. Each child is entirely responsible for his own belongings, even the smallest children. No valuables allowed, nothing that might be sold, or you could have your things confiscated, and be turned back."

"Terrific, you'd hear a knock on the door and it'd be me." Marianne ran to the bedroom door and rapped on it sharply. She turned round dramatically, saw her mother's stricken face and said, "I don't know why I'm behaving like this. I can't seem to help it. Sorry."

"I know, my darling," said Mrs. Kohn. "Let's start again."

Finally they decided on: hairbrush, comb, toothbrush and toothpaste. Dressing gown and slippers. Three pairs of socks. Three pairs of underwear – vests and underpants. Two sweaters – one red and one navy. Two blouses, two skirts. One pair of shoes, three handkerchiefs, paper and envelopes, and a German/English dictionary.

"You'll wear your brown lace-up boots and your Star of David

84

like you always do, under your blouse. And, of course, your winter overcoat. England is very cold and damp, I'm told."

"What about my new dress – surely there'll be special occasions in England?" Marianne stroked the velvet skirt of her party frock.

"I could make room, but you'd have to wear more underwear on the journey. That would leave us enough space."

"Mutti, do you want me to die of heatstroke before I get there?" said Marianne, and this time she was only half joking.

"In December? You exaggerate so, Marianne."

Marianne said, "Are we going to have a fight?"

"Of course," said her mother, "isn't this a normal day? Come here, wicked daughter, and give me a hug. I forgot something. Fold your dress in tissue paper. We'll manage."

As soon as her mother left the room, Marianne squashed her teddy bear down the side of the case. He was quite thin after years of hugging. She couldn't go to sleep without him.

Marianne shut the case, then walked round the room with it, testing its weight. She smiled at her mother as she came back into the room. "I can manage this really easily; it's not heavy at all," she fibbed.

"Here are ten marks. The Nazis won't allow you to take more than that out of the country. It's very little, but as soon as you are settled, I'll try to send you more. Now put five marks in your purse and I'll pin the other five inside your coat pocket. Just to be on the safe side."

"You sound just like Emil's mother," said Marianne, and stopped. She remembered Ernest. She hoped she'd never see *him* again.

"Here is your passport. You'll need to show it when you cross the Dutch frontier. The ss will come aboard, or perhaps the Gestapo. Don't be afraid. Your papers are in order – you are on the list of children permitted to travel. Marianne, you know what I'm going to say."

"Be careful, don't draw attention to myself, be polite. I know," said Marianne.

"No smart remarks. You always make jokes – they could be misunderstood," said her mother.

Marianne looked at her passport. She clutched her stomach. "Oh, the pain, it's awful." She bent over in agony.

"Oh, my darling, what is it? Appendicitis?" Mrs. Kohn helped Marianne to the bed. "Sit down and tell me where it hurts."

"It's just the picture – I look so awful. It's even worse than my school one. And look at that dreadful red J. Do they think I'll forget I'm Jewish?"

"Marianne, you see what I mean, you *have* to stop this playacting, at least till you get out of Germany. Once you're over the border, you'll be safe. Promise me to be sensible."

"Of course I promise. I'm just nervous. My lips will be sealed. I could even put a handkerchief over my mouth and pretend I've just come from the dentist and can't talk. Alright, I'll stop. Just teasing."

Mrs. Kohn shook her head in mock despair. "You won't like this either, I'm afraid, Marianne." Mrs. Kohn put a cardboard label tied to a piece of string around Marianne's neck. "We have been told all children have to wear this as identification. See, I've printed your name, destination, and your number – 206."

"I feel like a piece of luggage. Let's hope I don't get lost."

Mrs. Kohn said, "We'll put all your things in the hall. We must leave at six in the morning. It's a long way to the railway station."

Marianne said, "If I have to listen to one more thing about tomorrow, I'll scream."

"But I haven't even told you about the boat that's waiting at the Hook to take you to England."

Marianne continued quite seriously, "Please, let's not talk about tomorrow anymore. Do you know what I'd like to do? Bake a chocolate cake for your birthday and eat it tonight."

"Before we do that, I have to give you one more thing. Don't groan, it's an early Hanukkah gift. It's from Vati too, and we want you to open it now."

Marianne undid the daintily wrapped parcel. Her mother had glued paper candles on the tissue paper. For once Marianne took her time. She threw her arms round her mother's neck.

"I've so longed to have a copy of *Emil and the Detectives* of my own. I won't even peek at it until I'm in England. I'll save it, something from home to look forward to. Thank you a thousand times."

Mother and daughter went into the kitchen with their arms around each other.

· 17 ·

"We are not all the same"

Next morning at ten minutes to six, Marianne stood in the hall, dressed and ready to go, with the luggage label fastened around her neck. Her mother was in the kitchen, making a big lunch for Marianne to take on the train.

There was a knock on the door. Marianne opened it.

Ernest, dressed in the outfit he had worn on that first day when he arrived in Berlin from Freibourg, stood there. He was holding a small package. "I'm going back today," said Ernest hesitantly. "Home to Freibourg."

"I'm leaving too, in a few minutes," said Marianne. "I'm going to England."

"I bet it's a long way on the train," said Ernest. "Watch out for men in bowler hats."

They both started laughing, remembering their first meeting.

Ernest said, "Well, I just came to say good-bye. I brought you something." He handed Marianne an oddly-shaped package, wrapped in brown paper and tied with string. "You can open it when I'm gone."

A harsh voice called from downstairs, "Ernest, I forbade you to go upstairs again. Come down this minute." Ernest straightened up, his arm flew out and, for a dreadful moment, Marianne thought he was going to say, "*Heil Hitler.*"

Ernest stuck out his hand; Marianne took it. They shook hands.

"Good luck, Marianne. Perhaps you'll come back to Berlin someday."

"Good-bye. Thanks Ernest," said Marianne.

Ernest ran downstairs, two steps at a time. The door of Number One closed behind him. Marianne went back inside her apartment and shut the door. She ripped open the parcel. Inside was Ernest's most precious possession – the motor-horn. On the back of a postcard with a view of Unter den Linden, Ernest had written:

Berlin, December 1, 1938
We are not all the same.
Good-bye Marianne
From your friend
Ernest

Marianne put the motor-horn in her coat pocket, and the postcard in her purse. Mr. Altmann had been right. Ernest was one of the brave voices.

"Who was that?" asked her mother.

"A friend," said Marianne. "He came to say good-bye."

· 18 ·

The Train

In the subway all the way to the railway station, standing wedged tightly against her mother, Marianne was aware of Ernest's present in her coat pocket. She repeated the words on the card silently to herself:

"We are not all the same."

They comforted her a little.

Now and again, Mrs. Kohn smiled gently at Marianne. It was wiser not to speak in the compartment crowded with early-morning workers. Someone might be listening and cause problems.

It was a relief to get out at last into the frosty December air. Marianne looked at her watch: 7:15 A.M. precisely. There was still almost three-quarters of an hour left. She needn't say goodbye yet.

"Please let me carry my suitcase, Mutti. I have to get used to being on my own." Mrs. Kohn didn't argue, she just squeezed Marianne's fingers and then handed her the case. They walked through the vast pillared doorway of the Berlin railway station. Immediately they were assaulted by sights and sounds of such confusion, noise, and terror that Marianne's questions were left unspoken.

The glass and steel roof of the huge terminal was high and cavernous. The daylight, which entered through the tall windows, seemed pale in comparison to the blaze of electric light that lit up every sad face. There were seemingly endless railway tracks, which Marianne knew sent trains all over Europe. SS guards stood every few paces. Some had powerfully muscled watchdogs beside them. Marianne was afraid to look at the dogs. She thought, 'If one jumps up at me, it could tear out my throat.' Their leather collars gleamed as brightly as their masters' glossy boots.

Once they'd passed through the barrier, Marianne and her mother found the platform crammed with children of all ages. Some in brand-new clothes, others wearing hand-me-downs, or so many layers that their faces were red and sweating.

Parents, grandparents, aunts, uncles, older and younger brothers and sisters stood in mournful clumps, trying to create a small, last-minute zone of comfort to make their grief at being parted more private.

Marianne and her mother walked along the platform, jostling for a place to be alone for a minute.

"The journey won't be easy, Marianne," said her mother. "Have you got your lunch?"

"Right here, Mutti. I won't starve," said Marianne. Mrs. Kohn straightened Marianne's label.

"How will you all manage with only three supervisors amongst so many children? And they have to come back to Berlin as soon as you reach the Dutch border. They promised the authorities, and if they don't keep their word, the Nazis won't allow any more children to leave. Oh, Marianne!" She suppressed a sob.

"Mutti, please stop worrying. I'm almost twelve years old. I can look after myself. There are children much younger than me going by themselves." Marianne looked at the faces behind the barrier. "I thought perhaps, I hoped, you know, that Vati might come to see me off too. I know he can't. I understand," said Marianne. "Tell him . . ." The rest of her words were lost in a hiss of steam as the big green and black and chrome train pulled into the station.

"I'll tell him, darling. I'll tell him good-bye for you."

A voice over the loudspeaker announced, "All Aboard." Pandemonium, as people pushed and scrambled to get their children on board and settled.

"The adults have to wait behind the gate, Marianne. Be quick," said Mrs. Kohn.

The station clock pointed to four minutes to 8:00 A.M. Trains always left punctually in the Third *Reich*. Marianne grabbed her case and hurled it onto a wooden seat by the window to reserve her place, then jumped down the high train steps to spend her last precious two minutes with her mother.

The train filled with children. Last-minute advice was shouted and whispered. Marianne saw a little boy jump into his mother's arms, saw her carry him away through the gate and out of the station.

"I love you, Mutti, I'll write as soon as I get to England. I'll be alright, I promise I'll be alright. I'll remember everything you told me."

"I have to go. We are not allowed to remain on the platform. I'll wave from behind the barrier till you're out of sight. Never forget how much we love you." Mrs. Kohn put her hand to her daughter's face. She kissed her cheek and hurried to stand with the other relatives.

Marianne's eyes were so full of tears she had to feel her way back onto the train. She lifted her suitcase onto the rack. The station guard slammed the compartment doors one by one. The noise echoed along the train.

Just before the guard reached their compartment door, a woman threw in a rucksack, then lifted a little girl and stood her beside Marianne. "Please look after her. Thank you." She kissed the child's hand and moved away without looking back.

'I'm not going to talk about today,' Marianne promised herself, 'not even when I'm old and have children of my own. No one is going to believe this happened to us.'

The train whistled shrilly, and Marianne and the other children crowded round the window again to wave, until the station

was left far behind. They took off their coats and scarves. It was a
relief to be away from the tension of the station. One of the boys
put the little girl's case on the rack for her.

"Thank you," she said. "I'm Sophie Mandel. I'm seven." They
all introduced themselves. Werner was the tallest of the three
boys; Heinz was the one who had helped Sophie.

"I'm Liselotte Blum," said a pretty girl of about fourteen.

"And I'm Brigitte Levy." A plump, dimpled face smiled in a
friendly way at all of them.

"I'm Josef Stein," said a curly-haired boy who looked about the
same age as Ernest.

For the first time Marianne looked at the small girl with short,
fair hair and dark eyes, sitting on the edge of the seat. She held a
doll. Her legs, in wrinkled brown stockings and tightly laced
brown ankle boots, swung far above the floor. Marianne smiled at
the child who had been put in her charge. "I'm Marianne Kohn,"
she said.

They all stared at each other, not feeling a bit shy, and there
was almost a holiday feeling in the air.

Brigitte said, "What an adventure."

Heinz said, "I'm starved. I was too nervous to eat breakfast. I'm
going to eat my lunch now." They all opened their lunch bags.
Everyone had a thick sandwich and a piece of fruit. Marianne
had cake as well. They cut up their sandwiches and shared.
Marianne sliced her chocolate cake into seven pieces with Josef's
penknife, and Sophie contributed an orange from the pocket of
her blue and white striped dress.

After lunch they practised English phrases, and taught Sophie to say, "The sun is shining." The compartment smelled of orange peel and chocolate. They were hot and thirsty, and dozed off after awhile. Sophie slept soundly, her head on Marianne's shoulder.

The train sped on toward the border.

· 19 ·

Inspection

They woke up when the train stopped. Werner said, "We must be close to the Dutch frontier." He looked out of the window. "Gestapo coming on board. Sit up straight. Don't say or do anything."

The children sat motionless, waiting.

The Gestapo entered the carriages, one officer to each compartment. "Passports."

The children held out the precious documents. Marianne put her hand in Sophie's coat pocket and, thank goodness, the passport was there. She held it out with her own. The officer barely glanced at the pictures. He pointed to the luggage racks.

"Open up," he ordered.

They put their suitcases on the seat for inspection.

The Gestapo officer, with a quick movement, overturned each case and ran his black-gloved hand through the contents. He pulled out Werner's stamp album and flicked carelessly through the pages, then put the album under his arm. When he opened Marianne's suitcase, he pushed the party dress aside, reached down inside the suitcase, found Marianne's bear, and hit the cherished toy sharply across his knee.

What was he looking for?

Marianne looked down on the dusty compartment floor, where her dress had slipped out of its tissue-paper wrapping. Under the green velvet sleeve, a small white envelope, with her name written in her mother's neat lettering, protruded.

Silently, without seeming to move, Marianne stepped forward. Her foot covered the paper. Marianne tried to steady her breathing; willed herself not to tremble.

The officer opened the back of Liselotte's framed picture of her parents, stepping deliberately on Brigitte's clean white blouse, which had fallen to the floor. Josef's prayer shawl was thrown aside. Sophie's doll was grabbed, its head twisted off. Then the officer turned the doll upside down and shook it.

Sophie cried quietly.

Marianne saw Josef clench his fist and open his mouth. She knew he was about to say something that would anger the officer. In desperation, she curled her fingers around the motor-horn in her pocket and squeezed. In the small space, the sound was as deafening as an explosion.

The children watched. No one moved. Josef's eyes met Marianne's for a moment. She looked down.

A second pair of black boots appeared at the door of the compartment.

"Enough," said a voice. Marianne looked up. The Gestapo were leaving the train.

Josef smiled his thanks. Marianne's knees were trembling so hard she had to sit down. The train whistle blew, and the locomotive began to pick up speed.

Brigitte said, "Sophie, we're in charge of the doll hospital. *Fraülein*, please hand your doll over for repairs."

Sophie smiled.

With careful fingers, Brigitte twisted the doll's head back onto the neck and said, "Good as new," and returned the doll to Sophie.

Only then was Marianne sufficiently under control to pick up the envelope and take out the letter it contained. It read:

"My dearest daughter,

"You will be far away from me when you read this letter. It is so hard to let you go. I watched you sleeping last night as though you were still a small baby. I wished I could change my mind and keep you here, but that would be too selfish.

"You are going to a better, safer life. Here, there might be no life at all. One day you will understand why I had to let you go. If only we had more time together. Someone else will lengthen your clothes, buy you new shoes, tie your hair. Did it grow into curls as you always hoped it would? I miss you already. I will miss having to nag you for coming in late. I will miss complaining about your messy room, or you not doing your homework. I will miss your first grown-up party. Will you still love to dance?

"Please try to understand, Marianne, why I must miss all your growing up, all these special things. Because I love you, I want to give you the very best life there is, and that means a chance to grow up in a free country. Here there is only fear.

"I pray that you, and all the children whose parents send them away, will find loving families. I will think of you every day, and wish for your happiness, and that you will grow up into a good and honorable person.

"Wherever you are, wherever I am, at night we will be looking at the same sky.

Always, your loving Mutti."

Marianne was crying. This time she did not attempt to hold back her tears. "It was a letter from my mother," she said.

Werner blew his nose noisily. Josef turned his back and started throwing all his stuff back into his suitcase. Marianne watched him spend a long time folding his prayer shawl before clicking the lid of his suitcase shut. Liselotte and Brigitte had their arms around each other.

"I need to go to the bathroom," said Sophie, and held out her hand to Marianne.

When they got back, the others had repacked Sophie's and Marianne's things as well as their own.

The train steamed into a station – a Dutch station! The children on the train went wild. Windows were pulled down, hats and handkerchiefs waved, voices shouted greetings, strangers shook hands.

Women, wearing clogs, handed drinks and bags of food through the open windows.

Werner took in a huge basket full of white rolls, butter and cheese. There were even bars of chocolate for each of them. A note with GOOD LUCK was pinned to a clean, white napkin which covered the food. The compartment which minutes before had been tense, angry and tearful, hummed with laughter and thanks.

"Good-bye."

"Safe journey."

"Thank you."

The train passed through the neat Dutch countryside, and the sound of children's voices floated out of the windows, over the dikes and windmills, into the December skies. A train of sadness had been transformed into a holiday train.

Josef began the song, sung at the end of the Passover meal – the festival that celebrates the flight of the Jews from Egypt and the journey to the Promised Land. What did it matter that it was the wrong time of year? Weren't they an exodus of children?

Just as they began to sing the verse about the Holy One, "Blessed is He," the train stopped.

· 20 ·

The Ship - into the Future

The train emptied its load of children. Eager hands helped them down the steps, patted cheeks, found luggage, tucked chocolate bars into pockets, and pointed them towards the quay. Tiredly, they filed out of the small, clean, train station and into the cold December darkness of the cobbled square.

"My face stings from the wind," said Sophie, running to keep up with Marianne. "Where is the sea? Why isn't it here?"

"I can smell it, mmm, like herrings. We'll be there very soon." The long line of children followed the path down to the water.

"My case feels as though there are rocks in it," Marianne said to Sophie. "Can you still manage your rucksack?"

A ripple of sound, like seagulls calling each other, shivered through the weary procession. "The ship, the ship." Everyone took up the cry.

There, looming up out of the darkness like a great white bird against the gloomy December sky, was the boat. They could see it clearly, shifting impatiently on the waves, eager to be free of its moorings.

Marianne said, "It's called De Praag. Look, the name's painted on the side."

Some men in uniform waved and came running toward the straggling line. The small travelers stopped moving. Sophie grasped her doll more tightly. Marianne took her free hand.

Could it be a hoax? The Hoek of Holland. That reminded Marianne of the hooks of the swastika. Were the Gestapo going to drown them?

A whisper filtered through from the front of the line. "They're friends, pass it on. Sailors from the ship. The uniforms are British."

A cheer went up from the ship as the first children reached the wooden gangway and climbed excitedly on board. Marianne stood leaning over the ship's railing, looking out into the darkness. So many children still to come. How had the train held them all? So many parents sitting tonight with empty places at the table.

Ruth out there in that friendly country. Would they meet again one day?

Other children joined her at the railing, wanting one last look at land before they sailed, at all they were leaving behind.

"What are you thinking about, Marianne?" asked Sophie beside her.

"My father said to me once, 'We can be together in our thoughts, even if we don't live together.' I'm remembering, storing up so I won't forget."

The ship's engines began to hum steadily. The last child was on board. Sailors removed the gangway. The ship started to move.

"At last. We're going. Tomorrow we'll be in England," said Marianne.

"What a long journey," said Sophie.

"Yes, but we're almost there."

The ship sailed on, into the darkness, into safety, into the future.

AFTERWORD

Good-bye Marianne is a work of fiction based on factual events.

The De Praag arrived at Parkstone Quay, Harwich, England on the morning of Friday, December 2, 1938 at 5:30 A.M. On board were the children of the first *Kindertransport*. There were to be many more, organized by the British government, and helped by the Children's Refugee Movement and dedicated people who offered aid of every kind.

Irene Kirstein Watts lived at Richard Wagnerstrasse 3, Charlottenburg, Berlin, Germany until she was sent to England by *Kindertransport* on December 10, 1938. She was then seven and one-half years old.

The transports continued until the outbreak of the Second World War in September, 1939. The *Kindertransportes* were a lifeline that rescued 10,000 children from Europe.

The Nazis murdered one and one-half million children under the age of fifteen.